YOU AND I MAKE SENSE

PRAVARA KALANGI

Copyright © Pravara Kalangi
All Rights Reserved.

This book has been self-published with all reasonable efforts taken to make the material error-free by the author. No part of this book shall be used, reproduced in any manner whatsoever without written permission from the author, except in the case of brief quotations embodied in critical articles and reviews.

The Author of this book is solely responsible and liable for its content including but not limited to the views, representations, descriptions, statements, information, opinions and references ["Content"]. The Content of this book shall not constitute or be construed or deemed to reflect the opinion or expression of the Publisher or Editor. Neither the Publisher nor Editor endorse or approve the Content of this book or guarantee the reliability, accuracy or completeness of the Content published herein and do not make any representations or warranties of any kind, express or implied, including but not limited to the implied warranties of merchantability, fitness for a particular purpose. The Publisher and Editor shall not be liable whatsoever for any errors, omissions, whether such errors or omissions result from negligence, accident, or any other cause or claims for loss or damages of any kind, including without limitation, indirect or consequential loss or damage arising out of use, inability to use, or about the reliability, accuracy or sufficiency of the information contained in this book.

Made with ♥ on the Notion Press Platform
www.notionpress.com

Dedicated to my Parents and Brother.

You and I make sense

---·♡·---

Mumbai, Bandra - 16th Sept

A fortnight of celebration with colors, music, and happiness had painted the walls and roads of Mumbai. It's been already a week and the city has calmed down from its festival mood. Not just the city even the journey of my love has been brought to its shore. Days were very annoying, which had never been before the 'big day'. There was a deep silence within me when I had heard that mom was relieving 'A sense of pride, Sam's characteristics have strengthened the bond between the two families'. That moment I was filled with disturbing emotions. It's hard to be in the life of someone else when you have the love of your life who wants to hold you for the rest of life. I have gone through a broken experience of 'love & hate' and 'low & high' feelings which brought a clash of feelings towards my relationship. But all that was in the past and now, I know, I am holding the love that is destined to be mine.

Mom touched my back 'Sonu beta, why are you still not in the traditional raiment? It's time for you to become a Dulhan. You should cherish your special day that would lighten up our mood for this grand festive ceremony. Your dear brother has chosen to make an appearance in dhoti from Isha's couture to accompany Sam whilst giving him a warm quilt in the event. So a big appreciation to my saccharine son.'

With a loving smile, she showed the bracelet that would be given to her son-in-law as a ritual. And thrived to arousal while taking out the emerald, ruby, and diamond stones embellished mesmerizing pieces of jewelleries that had been passing on from generations to our family's heritage. She over displayed in front of me to put on those ancestral ornaments. Without an iota of doubt, any girl would go crazy and get tempted by the grandeur of those jewelleries as unobvious I did.

With a feeling of upset I asked her in a low voice, 'Mom, I will soon be in an ethnic shape, but where is Isha? She hasn't made her presence so far'.

There will be the presence of an unspoken tension that will continue till the last hours to the wedding if you don't have any clue on your bestie's attendance. What if she doesn't turn up for the marriage?

Lately, a phone call came from her, and to my pleasure, she was with the groom and was guiding him about how to drape beautifully articulated dhoti in a typical Indian style. She recommended him from her fashionably handcrafted designer spirits.

She conveyed, 'Listen, sweets, your win over the disputed thought of choosing the right man is on his way and is all set to tie the knot. So get ready to knock him out with your slaying bridal looks'.

She is very special in my life. It's not simply a mere good friendship that both of us share but a very strong bond going beyond that. A sure justifier for playing multiple roles of being a good friend, strong supporter, cousinship, well-wisher, secret admirer, trouble giver, and making you feel the 'yaari' means everything. She was born to a mediocre family with independent and versatile thoughts. A specialized and accomplished fashion designing graduate from prestigious NIFT, Delhi, whose urge to carry out style and trend is phenomenal.

A week before my wedding, my dad said, 'Beta, to every father, their daughter is their precious little princess and they surely want nothing less than a perfect prince as a son-in-law. But they forget to note that we live in a period where it is more important to find the right person than a perfect person, the one who could make their princess feel special, the one who could fil challis of love, the one who completes her. With your love back in your arms, I feel like you made me realize that dream and my heart is finally at ease and joy. Bless you, beta'.

Days were very annoying before this big day. In this contemporary times, it is rare to find a person whose life is meaningful with you and also to possess the love for each other that is uniting both of you. You feel blessed when things like this happen. I looked back to console my setbacks. It was early morning. I was on a fitness regime.

I had to gain composure to just finish off my sweat-shed schedule. My trainer asked me , 'Why didn't you show your usual dedication in today's work out?'

I replied, 'Well, I have a party in the evening.' She showed a sweet smile while leaving.

I opened my closet to check for the best outfit that will fit, but within seconds I realized that nothing seemed so attractive which could match the party spirit even though the closet was bursting with clothes. 'Shit man! I don't have clothes for' Before completing the sentence, my roomies chord in a chorus, resonating Diya's dominant comment, 'Enough! Don't ever dare to say no clothes, blah! blah! blah!' I was wondering, did I complain?

My only apprehension was for proper attire to have an awesome look for the celebration. After some relentless struggle, I found a glittery golden semi-formal gown that came with frill sleeves and fitted bodice at the waistline.

They agreed when I said, 'This will be perfect!'

I was happy while getting dressed up. At that moment, a phone call had come from my dad which remained unattended as I was running late so thought to speak him while driving. Metro cities such as Bangalore have huge traffic congestion. And to avoid this, people should start quite early to reach their destinations at the time or has to suffer. Well, I'm one amongst those who don't want to be a victim of traffic. But today I am quite late and my dear one is already there at the venue. Stuck at the signal, I dialed dad's number.

*****

He asked 'I can hear a lot of vehicle honking, where are you?' I replied, 'Dad, I am heading to a club.'

With a concerning voice, he said, 'Ok. Be safe and reach your room early, I repeat reach early and call back'.

I replied, 'Will do that.'

I arrived, 'Ikya is holding a rose bouquet and waiting for someone.' I spoke to her, 'Hey baby, why are you still here? Let's go.'

She reacted, 'This is for my friend.'

Accompanying her, I also waited for almost half an hour. But then it started to drizzle so had to go inside. Soon we were thrashed into heavy mob environment when we landed on the dance floor. Shakira's 'Whenever, wherever(Stereo)' was playing on with heavy beats that shoot our moods to high on moments. In the fringe of the crowd, and within her group of friends I was the only uncommon girl dancing with them. She happens to be my dearest ex-colleague, an outspoken lady with deep insights for affairs. She was very prompt in carrying out actions that were dealt instinctively by her. She expertise in reading people's mind. Her introspection can make you feel wonderstruck.

Suddenly she screamed slowing down her body moves 'look there', she exclaimed with shocking expression.

I saw a fierce lady who looked like a bodybuilder with heavy muscles at the arms and thighs. In dark, if you see that kind of broad physical personality you will surely get super scared. I asked if that person is her friend.

She denied saying 'Will tell you just come with me.'

Oh God, I couldn't believe such a big human girl can exist. Ikya greeted her and spoke 'What a strange coincidence meeting you here twice. Wow, finally you build the body. I am surprised to see your transformation so quickly'.

I have no idea what was happening between them. Watching my face Ikya said 'You know, her motto was to look like a well-built guy. Damn easily she did it, awesome right? Last time I met her in this same place. She had an average built body.' Though I didn't find anything exciting in that I said 'yes of-course.'

I don't prefer to make friends just at first meet. I am very choosy and don't become close unless I feel comfortable with the person unlike to Ikya's personality.

The conversation with the 'big woman' went on for sometime. She described the nature of typical men and wants to stand out amongst dominated men and prove to them that women are strong both physically and emotionally. And she showcased some boxing exercises for fun. All of a sudden one female stabbed on the biggie's face to her surprise, soon she fell.

Ikya immediately reacted 'Let's lift and make her straight.'

I was totally blank with what she just said. I looked at her wondering if that is possible? Ikya repeated to carry out the quick action. I said that it can't be done. At that time somehow lady Tyson got up on her own but was bleeding badly from nose and face was also distorted. Ikya's friends and we both have managed to take her to hospital. We were tightly packed inside the car and there was severe press between us. And in this course of time, I was getting calls, multiple times from Dad. I told to myself, It was 11 PM in the night if I pick he will panic so it will be wise to neglect his calls till I reached my room.

Once home, I called him with the thought of getting screwed up but the scenario was different which I didn't expect. I began by apologizing, 'Sorry Dad, I have missed out to call you and inform.'

He said 'I didn't bother you for this, there is something else I wanna tell you and was trying to reach you. In the evening you were in a hurry so now I can talk to you.'

I was rolling on my bed struggling to sleep, thoughts were swirling like traffic in my mind while recollecting the words of dad 'Don't be stubborn. You know he is from a well-mannered family. You don't have to really hesitate to meet him. This would be a good alliance'.

In this regard, Dad sounded like I should be having preoccupied thought that a guy from reputed family supposedly needs to be good. Whatever would be the outcome I had to acknowledge him to meet this strange person.

The next day I woke up before my usual time for a Sunday morning. I saw Diya putting her baggage out to travel and left some stuff in hurry lastly sighing good luck as she heard the discussion, the previous night. To get off this weird feeling of meeting an unknown person I wanted to talk to Isha, even though she didn't have mastery over all this but surely she would be the right one with whom to discuss the matter.

'Heyyyyy' Isha's tone led to snide. 'How come you have time, was that a wrong dial? I am back from London for Chotu's thread ceremony'.

I reacted, 'Oh wow! How long is your stay? How come you gave no notice to me of your visit? Idiot, it's you who is obstinately busy'.

Actually, it's been a long time since we spoke. When she first said 'hello', I had a wonderful feeling to hear her voice while she continued, 'I have to tell you many things.' but I didn't give her a chance to say anything more as I conveyed my situation.

She mentioned 'Though the meeting is with the stranger, you are going to be on your first date. Let's make it special.'

I was briefed by Dad to be at Starbucks. That evening the hangout premises seemed to be somewhat uncanny. It might be because I had come to encounter an unusual happening. Although I arrived there much earlier than the discussed time, he was supposed to come at the scheduled time but he didn't. I hate people if they are not punctual.

Well, my mind was filled with questions. What to speak? What not to speak? How to behave? How to react?

Since I was left with no answers, I prepared myself to be very casual as always. Before I could prepare myself completely, he had come with a super cool look.

Hey, I'm Raj and forwarded his hand to me for a handshake. I also shook his hand.

There was absolute silence for a while. I can only hear my heartbeats.

I looked at my brother. He seemed comfortable. I thought 'really, didn't know how I'm gonna be throughout.'

Raj initiated the talk. He spoke to my brother 'So you were able to catch the flight from Mumbai and be here at the right time. Actually, I wanted to meet her alone but your dad said you would come along. So you have been troubled to travel'.

That time my brother's expression was so weird, which meant 'why the hell I am here'.

At many instances, Raj spoke to me as though he knew me so much. But I didn't feel the same towards him. My first impression lasted in my mind with dad's projection about this guy that he is a simple and casual person. During a couple of instances when he did good humor, I laughed louder putting my inhibitions aside. Slowly we both started to speak more. His interests were quite varied. He was keen on flying planes, sports, traveling, adventure, partying, hanging out with friends, a foodie and has an intrinsic value for culture and tradition. Before I could presume that he barely knows about me, he started sharing things. He knew much more than I expected.

I was quite impressed by the way he talked and leverages things. Sometimes you feel that you know the person very well even though you meet for the first time. It is because your thoughts and intrusions are the same.

Raj has two younger sisters. Being the eldest he adheres the responsibility. The youngest of the two sisters is privileged like a daughter that fascinated me the most.

After spending 4 hours, we left the place. They both accompanied to drop me at my place. While leaving he didn't take his sight off for a long time. I was feeling conscious but somewhere I sensed there was a magical connection. I reached my room and turned on lights.

'Hello Dad, Raj is a wonderful guy. There is no disappointment meeting him. I don't regret this happened.' And ended the call.

A week later I heard a familiar voice 'Almighty please open the door fast'.

I was thrashed inside soon after I did it. 'You portly, how much time you require to open the door.'

'You are alive?' I abused rather than saying 'how are you?' And I was not allowed to speak. Crazy lady, she grunted and then rushed to use emergency. I got her situation.

'Diya you planned for a long trip, then how come you are back so soon?

Did you really go? I asked.

She replied 'I am a mad girl right, just traveled to and fro'.

I started to laugh. She said 'By the way, how was the meeting with your guy?'

We hang up on call after I met him and told her that he was someone who likes masking out self-introductory speech. He likes people to be independent and a serene personality.

'My darling', she continued, 'We girls grace boys beyond what they actually are, you know you shouldn't do that. By the way, when was the last time you spoke to him?'

'The recent one was when he was traveling to New York.' 'What did he speak about?', Diya asked with curiosity.

'Since he arrived at the last minute to board the flight, we spoke only for some time and he said he would respond once he reaches.'

She looked into my eyes and said 'So, Miss Libra, your meeting with him is like a fairy tale. Let's see where it takes you'.

Diya said that she felt like a hungry devil and insisted that I cook something for her. She further said 'Seriously

I was bored with Italian dishes. We should prepare an Indian classic recipe'.

I asked 'Really! how come your tongue buds are craving for desi taste.'

While preparing the food, we were deep into talks. Suddenly she said 'Calm down the cutting sound', as she heard a beep tone beneath the oven. She handed over the mobile to me and said 'Reply to these flooding messages'.

I took the mobile and surprisingly exclaimed 'It is Raj'. He had texted 'Hey dear what's up?'

Since his first text, I confirmed him for someone else and replied to him saying 'I thought you are still flying and didn't land yet'.

He replied 'Hahaha I got your sarcasm. Actually, I wanted to catch up with you on the weekend for long hours but that went in vain. Hope you didn't feel bad for not being quick'.

Diya was also following our conversation so she responded to me 'Well ask him to go to hell'.

She snatched the mobile from me to reply on my behalf. In that hurry instead of sending 'go to hell,' she typed 'go too hot' and sent. He responded 'It's not hot in fact, it is freezing here.'

I sat on the floor as I couldn't control my laughter and pulled her down as well.

Diya texted back 'Something is wrong with the gadget, it is not encrypting exact emotion'.

Like an infinite loop, I continued to laugh.

*****

I then took hot soup bowl and went away from her, sat on the couch to chat with him. He texted 'You are so spontaneous.' (He might have thought I'm quick to respond unlike him)

He again texted, 'Sweetie, my younger sister complimented on your dressing style and finds you pretty in ethnic wear'. (Not sure where she has seen me).

I replied 'Awe that's sweet. Thank her from my side. How's she doing anyway.'

He continued 'She is doing awesome. In fact, I have to tell you the day when I first saw you, I was totally flattered. You were looking so fabulous and beautiful in the blue carbuncle studded attire. I couldn't take my eyes off you. You also carried a typical Indian girl look that day'. And he mentioned 'It's difficult to type, can I call you?'

I replied 'Call now?' (I questioned him but he took it as my reply).

He reverted, 'Yes will do that' and immediately, I received an incoming call.

My voice became like the sound of a squirrel. So I had to cover up that saying 'I had a long conversation with my friend so might be due to that my voice was strained.'

He responded 'Oh. Who is she?'

I asked him a different question to cover up that, saying 'How is your family?'

He said 'They all are doing fantastic. My dad and Mom are in Canada holidaying. Both my sisters, Shiny and the little one are in India'.

That's all, he had finished talking. What should I ask him to continue the conversation? No option was left, so I repeated to check on his family. I asked' Okay. Uncle and aunt must be enjoying a nice time. So they have come from India and are with you.

He responded 'No, I'm with them for 5 years.' I asked 'How come?'

He continued '27 years ago while my dad was working as sales head to one of the retail companies in India, he got an opportunity to work overseas. So the family had to shift to New York. A year later I was born. Though I was born here, I was brought up in India from the age of eight. And my two little sisters were born and brought up in India.

'Interesting!', I replied. 'So now you are working there?'

He responded 'Yes! Thought uncle(my dad) might have told you. That's the reason for our first meet didn't mention all these.'

I replied 'Not completely.' And I whispered to myself – Dad only mentioned that the guy is from a well-mannered family with good morals.

Raj then continued 'Okay cool. I'm a very liberal and friendly person that you can know of.'

He added 'Mom's influence is there upon all three of us. Her upbringing has restrained the instincts that made us disciplined. She doesn't want her kids to lack the traits of an Indian environment, I still have a clear picture of the way she squabbled with dad to allow us to study in India. Actually, for my higher studies, I had come here and now continuing with my job .'

I replied 'Great! You are lucky to have such a strong woman as your mom'.

He responded 'Yes, she is a truly strong lady and I am proud of that'. And he continued 'Hey I thought you know my background. To be frank, two days before we met, I spoke to your dad asking uncle to make it a casual meeting. And very special thanks to you. Without you, that meeting would have become pointless.'

Unexpectedly the call was put on hold and Raj resumed it after some time. He apologized and continued 'Last summer I had visited an Island located 400 km away to the south-east from the States. The beaches over there are fringed with palm trees and one can cherish the entire scenic beauty while walking on the island. It has bright blue waters sparkled with untainted purity. The ultimate enjoyment would be scuba diving in monsoons. So we friends are re-planning to visit the place again during the season of mist and haze .'

'Wow! ,' I exclaimed with joy. 'I wish to dwell to a spot around this place and continue staying there.'

He responded 'That would be a true paradise to live in.' Then he asked for an excuse to put our call on hold, and this time it was his parents.

Once the call continued I checked if we can connect tomorrow. I intended to know if he was busy at the moment. His response was very impulsive 'Yes will surely do it, probably we can talk at an earlier time than today'. He then continued 'My parent's gonna be in India after holidaying in Canada, so they are checking if I can join them'.

I replied 'Oh, is it? So when are you visiting?'

He responded 'I don't think so, at least in the last visit I had a reason to travel to India'.

I replied 'I think you were here for your cousin's wedding'.(He has mentioned this during our first meet)

He responded with confidence - 'Post that I did multiple visits but the last one is very special to me'.

I immediately checked 'When did our meeting happen?' (Though I knew).

He smiled and replied 'Your smart question is the answer, and my recent visit to India had to do with nothing else other than to meet you'.

There was silence for some time that froze the moment. He broke it saying, 'Whenever I consciously suffer from deep emotions and distant bonding I make a sudden appearance to friends and family. And that makes me feel good and happy'.He also extended his conversation, saying 'This is the only emotion that makes me weak as well.'

I replied 'You are calling yourself weak, I don't think so, in fact, you are making yourself strong by strengthening your emotion and can very much justify with the moments captured.'

He immediately asked me 'Can I say something'. I replied 'Ummm... Yea sure'.

He spoke to me 'You are way beyond what I thought of you. I don't want to hide behind words to express that my feelings for you are just flowing. You are simply awesome, awesome, and awesommmmme.' His words were so soothing but I was clueless on how to react to him. Slicing the topic, I said 'Ah! hey sorry forgot to mention that I have to shop some clothes for my friends fashion event'.

'Aahh! Wow! Sounds cool. So, are you in a rush to do shopping now? he responded.

I could feel the trough in his response. I responded 'Not really but.' 'You better do it as early as possible than keeping it for the last minute, we can catch up tomorrow, we will have an entire day to ourselves'.He interrupted me while I was about to complete the sentence.

Later that day, though I had no preplans but did some extravagant shopping and bought a few clothes. Suddenly woke up from sleep as my phone rang, voice stimulated with loving rush 'Hey dear sunshine? This is a wake-up call'.

This guy has taken the privilege of calling me dear and desires to own it. Smiling to myself, I replied 'Hey, I am still in bed, just give me some time.'

He replied 'Will stay online, when will you be back'.

Diya watching me spoke naughtily 'Kya baat hai? Aaj jaldhi aaye?

Washroom me pani nai tha ya phir kuch aur. Something is fishy ah ah!

I responded 'Grrrrrrr! calm down, idiot. He is waiting on the call and can hear us.

She annoyingly raised her tone 'Acha, then take your own time. I will engage him.'

I retorted 'Ishhh! Meri maa' with whispering voice to Diya and then continued with him - 'hello' But before his voice was heard I could listen tak-tak sound.'

He spoke 'You have to bear with me sorry about all this noise, I'm mashing potatoes for dinner.'

I said 'That's fine, as long as I can hear you.'

Diya with a discrete voice 'Hey, I can't hear you, man.'

He responded 'Your short and sweet replies never fail to put a smile on my face. I think someone is prompting from the back, can't hear. Who's that?'

I replied 'My friend Diya. She has an allegation on you.'

He responded 'Strange! What's that?'

I replied 'She feels, you troubled me for not being quick responsive.' He replied 'Is it? Want to know if it's your opinion too.'

I replied 'Of course my opinion reflects her. However, it turned out to be a myth after giving time in understanding you. To be frank, I must admit as an inherent person, you well placed yourself.'

He took pause and responded 'Dear, you hark back to Cera with whom I have a close association, she always remarks and also compliments me in this way for being like that.'

Some days are memorable. There was a blink on my phone. 'What are you doing babes.' I reacted while checking - 'Is this Raj?'

'Of course, it will be him. Were you expecting someone else?', Diya said with sarcasm.

Actually, it's the first time he called me babes and I felt like marking this moment. I sent him a girly happy smile. There was a call from him. I answered. He said 'I am very happy, you can ask for anything that you want from me now'.

I replied 'I don't want anything Raj. What are you doing by the way?' 'I was just preparing some documents for a meeting tomorrow.'

'Is it? Let me not bother you.'

'Babes, you are not at all a bother, in fact, you made this moment special and the drizzle outside makes it even more lovable for me and the work can wait.'

I asked 'Did you call me babes once again?'

He replied 'Yes you are that for me. What is it that makes you happy'. I replied 'Nothing in specific.' He insisted. So I said 'I like roses.'

Raj 'Roses?'

'Yeah! It shows how girls are gorgeous, lovable and protective.' He kept my call on hold. There was a blink again. When I checked it was him holding a bunch of red and white roses completely wet in rain having a selfie.

When he resumed, I reacted with a huge smile. 'Thanks for that, I really liked it.'

'If you smile like this, I will buy the garden for you. I smiled again you are too funny Raj.'

Initially, it was difficult for me to involve myself in a conversation but now, unknowingly it continued for hours without any interruption. Post the call, his two words dear and babes were lingering in my ears all the time. I didn't verbose much and hardly reacted to him, so was surprised when he mentioned I like your feminine talks. Though, it's a trivial remark.

******

Reached Home. Mid noon I exited the Airport gateway, in a little while have seen dad waving at me and then heard Raman uncle discoursing someone on phone 'Don't have to be silly, I have come a long way to receive you. Please stop being stupid'.

Uncle angrily complained to Dad 'Sam still continues to be impish and surprises me with his unexpected doing. A year back he dropped out from his education to form his music band since then he never visited India. Whenever we emphasize him to come he does things to befool me, so now I am pissed off by his behavior.'

While talking, they both went far ahead neglecting me, Dad all of a sudden from the other side shouted in an outraged voice, 'Watch the speeding vehicles and come here'. He gave a relieving expression after I did it. And then spoke to me worriedly 'You still didn't learn to cross the motorway. Always you need to be instructed to keep an eye on fasting vehicles.'

Raman uncle looking at me asked 'Are you scared of crossing'.

Dad replied 'Yes she is' and continued to say 'My daughter takes the vehicle round about the dividers and adjacent roads to avoid crossing. Sometimes she dropped us just in front of the entrance and juts the car into the building to overcome it. And she pacifies us stating it is easy to take the vehicle out and moves on.'

Immediately uncle freaked out laughing and gave pitiful expression to me. I screamed 'Dad this is not the time to make fun of me, we are getting churned in the scorching sun. Let's go from here'.

At home, Mom was dazed at my minimal shopping as she spread the stuff to pack my luggage. She worriedly said 'You might have come at least two days earlier so you could spend more time with us.

I replied 'Will do that after my return travel.' And acclaimed 'Mom, I sensed Raj to be a rationale for everything. He gives others their personal space and will let them be their selves. I feel we both have complementing personalities.'

She anxiously questioned 'How did you analyze all this?'

'We had brief talks and did chat conversations that make me feel so.' I replied She then continued 'Not sure why your dad never brought this topic to me post you guys have met.'

'You know Mom before we both could meet, Dad was absolutely sure and had a concrete opinion on Raj while I had conditional cognition.'

She smiled and responded 'Hope your dad continues with the same contemplation'.

Not sure why dad and mom didn't declare anything about him, especially dad as he is the person who is super fine with Raj and his family. However, I decided to poke him on this. Dad yelled at us, saying 'Can stay back if you are delaying more.'

Mom packed separate luggage for Isha and instructed us to be cautious and alert all the time. I went like a zombie and got into the vehicle. Dad asked 'Are you not excited to go. Should we back out?'

I responded 'No, Not at all.'

He reverted 'Then why are you this way?'

I mumbled 'This is heeding to Raj and I am feeling distressed as neither you nor mom opened up till now.'

Seeing me that way, Dad took a deep breath and responded 'Well should we declare to his parents that this alliance is ok for us?' Mom from the back, seated diagonally to me replied to him 'We can do that and proceed once she is back from London.' Then she showed thumps up that dad noticed and ignored.

Isha reached the Airport much earlier than us. She always instructs her family not to accompany her till the airport. This time they leapfrogged it and escorted her with uncovered emotions. Her entire family fraternity was present there. One can doubt as to how many of us are travelling tonight. Mom took Isha's niece in her arms and pampered her. Then pointed Isha over to the luggage and explained what all have been packed for her.

Isha meticulously addressed her family stating, 'How many times they repeat a single thing and do followups. Though I abide by the fact that they are very much worried. I know they had outpouring love, concern, and responsibility towards me but showing all these extensively was a hassle to me. Today there was a slight argument between us and I had to dictate that I can manage my stuff and told them please don't intervene.

Mom took the pride to explain to Isha, 'See you might be very independent in your living and best at managing self but for us, you are still young to persuade certain things. Though we have confidence in you sometimes we repeat a few things to ensure no fails and regrets occur. Even then, if you guys feel we elders are overdoing certain matters then just stay quiet and carry composure which is very essential.'

Mom extended her talk 'Don't overthink now, just spend the last remaining minutes with them.'

Isha conveyed 'Sure aunty, don't want to be emotionally surrendered while leaving.'

But then she turned to her family and spoke with smiles and giggles. At last, she took blessings from the elders followed by a long pitched bye to all. I too waved at my parents, while Mom was mentioning to Dad 'Since childhood Isha has been raised and supported by multiple hands, though she has the option to rely on others she chooses to do things by herself. Hardly dependent on anyone, she has unbelievable confidence to take up new challenges like our Sonu. They both have quite appreciable traits.'

Dad replied 'Of course, I agree'.

With nostalgic jiffies, Isha held my hand and said 'Dear let's jump from here and step into the zone of freedom.'

We landed in the early hours at the most happening city of fashion elites. Due to winters, the surrounding looked very mild and gloomy. On the other side of the glass openings, we could see dew drops which gave a hazy sight. Isha's neighbor Sania had come to pick us. Seeing our luggage she commented 'Heyyy will not skip opening a brand store for sure'.

Isha responded 'Haha, Let's do it.' And then I was introduced to Sania, 'She is my friend Sonu, a deadly yaari, I can always frolic.'

Sania to Isha 'Oh, I believe she is the one you spoke about.' and extended her hand to me for a handshake. I shook her hand looking into her blue eyes, I felt intrigued if she was of Irish origin.

Sania(with an Indian accent) spoke to me 'Actually I'm half Indian, mom hails from Ireland and dad is of Indian ancestry, basically a Konkani speaking person from Goa.'

Throughout the drive, Isha dozed off, while I started questioning Sania on her lifestyle and living. I was so surprised when she mentioned that her favourite hobby is to spend money, from a sleeping state, Isha suddenly spoke with a cracking voice 'Yeah, she pleasures to volatile wealth' and jerked her body when suddenly the vehicle was stopped for fuel. After that, we didn't stop anywhere and directly reached the homestay.

Isha mentioned 'Sorry guys, couldn't control my sleep, was damn tired and then made us hurry to do a makeover.' as she planned to meet Stella, an international fashion stalwart and style critic.

We walked into the world of fashion mania, where you can find models who are moving all over like dolls, looking very attractive and beautiful. Isha had designed feather fringe long gowns with stones embedded in them in various patterns. Every design is so very detailed and unique with rare shades of fabrics. Isha knew that Stella would be at the Wardrobe section so she took us midst a slender path on either side of which you will find art galleries and statues that are beautifully carved with accessories. Sania replicated most of the postures and posed in front of the statues.

Isha had to come back to us running as we could not be seen after half the way, she took her designs from us and commented after watching Sania's perfect pose 'Hello try for modeling, will recommend you to Stella.'

Then Sania forced out from her static pose and stated 'I am fine if you are providing me an additional meal in a day.' Isha with a funny gesture, stated 'Will throw you out of this World, let me meet Stella and come.'

We could hear Stella talking to Isha, 'Absolute grandeur designs, looking forward to all these to be presented. Though it's your first international event, you gonna grip the show.' She addressed event organizers to facilitate trial sessions to the models.

Italian and Persian models tried Isha's collections, and they appeared to be very hot and sizzling. Almost everyone carried a vibrant look. Once they had put on the dresses, Isha knitted the clothes as per their body measurements. Sania whispered something in my ears while she saw Isha approaching us, I soon laughed and said, 'You are too funny dear, how can you say that.'

She checked with us and remarked, 'Heyyy idiots, what's that.' Sania with sulk eyes, 'It's a prank, we are just playing around.'

Isha responded, 'I don't think so, seeing me there was a halt to whispering. I will not leave you guys, you have to say what is it.'

Sania then said 'Actually, there was a lady along with you coming to this side, from far she seemed like a man with trimmed hair cut so whispered to Sonu he is very fortunate to be surrounded by plenty of girls, full-on entertainment.'

Isha replied, 'Are you guys talking about Stella.'

Sania and me together, 'Is she S..., freak man, she is just behind you now.'

Stella handed over the event schedule to Isha and stated 'Your designs would be exhibited first, ensure that everything is well planned for the event to go smoothly and all things are taken care beforehand.'

Sania gave a suspicious look to Isha as to whether Stella had heard our conversation, then Isha made an epic introduction to Stella. 'She is my close buddy Sania who is massively prone to sophisticated styling and art, always set to new fashion adaptations. In many instances, she has enlightened me on good-quality fabric hue and designs. In fact, my previous designs were mostly executed by her.'

Stella was very much impressed and proclaimed 'Then I do recommend Sania to endorse your designs, she is the right person who can be launched in the best possible way. This event should be the ultimate platform for both of you to showcase your talents.'

Sania gave a meagre smile to Isha while responding to Stella 'Well it's a great opportunity and privilege to be part of such a magnificent happening'.

Stella hugged both of them saying, 'Wishing you guys good luck and will be longing to see you both at the event.'

Being only observant, I thoroughly followed their conversation. There was no exchange of talks between us for quite some time.

Isha broke it and stated 'This will yield a feeding for our entire life and not just an additional meal in a day.'

Sania replied, 'Phew, I'm still in shock the way you portrayed me to Stella, that lady is highly fascinated and wants me to launch your designs. Undoubtedly my ramp walk will go disastrous, I will surely end up clumsily carrying off myself, either dropping down the feathers, clinging to the gown or get blown away with it like a swan.'

Isha feeling concerned replied 'Hey, don't worry, will do trial performances till you are at ease with the outfit. Once you do mock ramp walk your confidence will rise. So just relax and don't be conscious of anything.'

Sania spoke woefully 'I'm still unsure about the outcome, can refurbish my thoughts over a cup of coffee.'

With fast pace we entered a sidewalk cafe, it had glass fence outside and inside for space separation. There was evening jazz playing on with the thrashing sound, during dance trumpet few couples screamed crazily. The ambience and liveliness gave us a wonderful experience.

Sania placed an order for three black cappuccinos and mentioned to us 'How to prepare for the event.'

Isha: 'I'm there to take care, repeated with the twitching pitch I'm there to take care.'

I patted her checking. 'What happened? Are you fine?'

Isha was gazing at her mobile while the phone rang, she picked it up and spoke in a steady posture 'Chris, I'm hanging out with friends. Will call back.'

Isha continued 'Senorita, it's not a worry at all, we gonna compile every craft with sensibility and creativity. Even there is a huge scope to override the competition. So I recommend you to enjoy the proceeding moments and be on the fun take. And then she extended her talk while going through the event schedule, 'Let's go to Morgan's place tomorrow and do Jungle visit.'

Sania responded like she is in trauma, 'Are you serious, how about my rehearsals for the event?'

Isha, 'Chill, Go easy on yourself, we can line-up from the day after.'

Sania with a quacking voice, 'Ahem ahem, can I still anticipate an additional meal?'

Looking at her spasm, Isha and I guffawed insanely.

Sania with concern remarked, 'Guys stop this, people around are watching us.'

Still, we continued to roar with laughter and we were forced by her to move out from there.

Driving back home Isha spoke 'Sania please stop making faces. I can't laugh anymore.'

Sania on high spirits spoke to Isha 'Why did you poise to Stella that I suggest you on clothing and styling. I always wear craggy clothes and never have an impulse for fashion. You and her supreme thought of elevating your designs with me to international standards is the sole reason for my intended facial expressions.'

'Shit man!' Isha stopped the car suddenly due to vehicle break down. Though we gave a hard push from the rear end but couldn't make it start. Sania in a muck sweat, remarked, 'This classic Chevrolet is completely dead, can't move an inch'.

Isha said, 'Let's walk, anyways we are just a few miles away from where we stay.'

On the way, Isha edified about ramp walks and body languages. She explained all supermodels have distinctive styles and do branding exercises. In modeling, personality is the main promo to create space for yourself and appreciated Sania, saying 'this will do' when she did some commendable walk.

Isha suddenly dialled to Chris and spoke, 'Take back your car, it is no more functional.'

Sania checked 'What did he say?'

Isha's reply was harsh, 'I didn't wait for his response, and ended the call.'

Sania sighed to me, 'Looks like Isha is upset for some reason, gently handle her, I will see you guys tomorrow morning.'

Isha wiping her face asked, 'Sania left, is it? Did she inform at what time we can start?'

I replied, 'No, she didn't mention the precise time but it sounded like early hours.'

Isha replied, 'That's fine, now let me take you to my World, my passion, and my dreams.'

She unveiled apparels from her wardrobe, I could see mesmerizing unusual flowing patterns bestowed with grandeur. All were irresistible forms, and one after the other, each one of those deeply fascinated me.

'Isha can I ask you something?', I asked.

She responded, 'Sweetheart I can hear your inner voice, pick any for the event.'

I replied, 'No not that, I feel something is bothering you badly. Before it pulls you down to emotional ail bring it out.'

Tears started rolling down her eyes. She held my hand tightly saying, 'I can't bear this anymore.' With a broken voice, she continued to speak sensitively, 'I know I cry like a kid. As you said some feelings are bothering me.'

I had never seen Isha get this much emotional. She is a lady with strong conviction. Well after some relaxation she prolonged to say 'A few months ago, I happened to meet Chris at my initial fashion events in Mumbai. Since he was the prime sponsor for the show, I was with him. Initially, he seemed to have no connection about the happenings, so I got slightly worried about how the event will go. Later, however, I was very impressed by the way he and his team organized and sequenced the entire event. It was novice nervousness from my side when the show had begun, but he surpassed it saying "Do not panic, your briefing and styling is very different, though you are a beginner your expertise don't portray that." Fortunately, without much challenges, the event did fairly good. A month later, for my next event, he braced me to the core, in fact, I got that opportunity through him. This time he was present at every small craftsmanship of mine. I was extremely impressed by the way he stayed and supported me.

Post the show, during party event, his co-sponsor Ankur grabbed the mic and announced, "Hi folks, I am more than just delighted to invite you all for the tour of the Londinium." in his Indo-Britain accent. Everyone was overjoyed but then came the muting moment when a presenter asked, 'Where is this Londinium?'. Ankur winked with a smile responding "That is our present-day London." They cheered as the celebration went on. Chris, still maintaining his calm posture turned to me and congratulated. He remarked, "You have done a fabulous job today, keep up the pace and I promise you will travel miles. So Miss Isha will you be visiting London?"

"Of course," I said, "I would love to" this was followed by his excited smile. From his face, my girly intuition could glimpse that something was fishy so planned on inquiring where he lives. With subtle expression, he replied "London" and emphasized with a smile. "I feel it's the best place for you to build your career, you can relocate there without any second thought."

I responded gently, "Well there is no denial in your statement, I need to advance on certain parameters to go for international canons.'

The moment was interrupted by Ankur, "Hey guys, whatsup? It's too early to be old so let's dance, the floor is on."

Chris poked him, "Bro I know these beats will not stop us from dancing but we are into something more important than this temptation. You fill in for me."

Then Ankur responded, "Can understand bro you too carry on."

Chris then continued to talk to me with absolute cool tempo, "I agree with you, sometimes quick executions do fetch better outcomes. This is my first time in India. I never had any plans to come here and do event investments. You never know what your destiny is. There is an unforeseen happening that will lead to an exciting turn.'

I smiled and said, "You are too realistic for a fortuity driven person." He replied, "If you feel so it can be." And mentioned "For some interesting reason, the first time this lashing music bang is annoying me'

and inquired with Ankur, "Bro suggest the best place nearby?"

Ankur smartly mentioned, "There is one Irani café, a clumsy place but famous for chai."

Chris then quickly checked with me, "Are you okay?"

Before I could say something he said, "Let's go." And I was caught off guard.

While we were moving out, I could hear Ankur's voice falling out of loud music beats. "It's not a comfortable place to hang out." But that didn't seem to bother Chris. Amidst a flowing crowd queued up to occupy space, Chris looked into me and spoke: "Huff, can't even breathe here." And I could see the stiffness in him. In this severe situation, he read to himself Ankur's text "Should we have to sponsor all the designers for the London trip."

Though not having the intention to know I eventually read it while he was about to respond. I resisted hard to laugh and checked with him while we sat, "What are you going to reply to him."

He then crazily responded to me, "My genius friend failed to understand whom to select so declared the trip for all the designers. There is no point discussing now." Then I mentioned indirectly, "Prolly he didn't get your intention based on your choices."

He couldn't control his laughter, "Not my problem. But now as there remains no other option, I believe he will have to solely bear all the expenses that will be incurred." And checking my expression he prolonged his talking, "Surely Ankur will be able to last this event as an investor."

His fun-filled talks made me laugh louder than ever. However, your moods are, irrespective of emotional eddies a strong lively feeling comes in his company, he became ultimately conscious and solemn while talking to his mom on the phone, "My visit to India was a complete disaster except for one special person."

After consistency check he offered me chai, saying, "You can relish the taste now, often due to my mom I ensure each ingredient is thoroughly mixed." I felt that something is interesting to know about this guy, 'So your parents reside in London?' I asked.

After a long pause, he eventually opened up on his front. His parents are an Indian couple and his ancestors date back to many centuries who migrated to the UK for a better living. Both his parents are famous industry stalwarts but got separated. His mom raised him as a single parent after the split. The most intriguing thing about him is, though he inherits million dollars as the familial heir, he chooses to stand on his own and earn by himself.

It was heavily raining on my drive back to mama's place and I wanted to inform my family, not to panic. However, the blank mobile screen made me realize that the battery had drained completely. He handed over his phone to dial-in and to my bad, I am poor in memorizing the #'s.

He checked with a concern, "Do you stay with your family here?"

We finally reached home. Well, this is my uncle's house and depending on my show and event schedules, I at times, come here. All cousins, mama, aunt, and dadi were silently watching us from the front space, peeping through the main gate. They exchanged a suspicious look with each other when I shook hand with Chris. Dadi to her curiosity came to see Chris closely and gave raging looks to him. He felt kind of odd and left stating, "Line up yourself at least a month before the trip."

I put my hand on dadi's shoulder and spoke to her, "What did you just do to Chris, he is a nice guy, don't form any bad impression about him."

My cousins were desperately trying to pull my legs. They started to say, "In this hammering rain you guys roamed the whole city skipping the event, can't believe how did your passionate career got neglected for him. At last, he mentioned 'trip' what's that?"

"Guys, please listen to me, he sponsored today's event and the outcome is fantastic. So all designers have been privileged for a visit."

They continued to tease saying that something is fishy, then I had to explain that if it was not for any intended reason. I wouldn't have been given the chance to travel. Thanks to Ankur for sponsoring all of us, it is supporting me. Dadi raised her tone with favouring words, saying, "Not so. She should be given the freedom of expression. But, I feel a tour should have a definite count of 10 days, 20 days, or 30 days but what is this. This trip will last at least for a month and also that guy sounded like this trip is exclusively for her.'

Again I couldn't bear this streamlined interrogation. So I said, "Let me call up all the other presenters and designers. They will explain everything."

From absolute silence and serious to funny faces, each one of them roared into uncontrolled laughter. Gradually Chotu, my cousin with a sweet voice said, "Dhidhi it's a prank."

Then dadi telephoned my parents and with the exaggerated tone, said, "Your daughter is awesome, wo humara naam roshan karegi. Usko London jaane ka chance mila. Wishing her good luck." And then she passed the phone to me, dad from the other end asked with a frisky voice, "When are you travelling then?'

Not sure if he didn't like what she spoke but I did reply, "This weekend, will be drifting from here."

A week later I have my flight to the United Kingdom. All fellow presenters are visiting only for a week. Dad checked with Ankur on our tour schedule. He nagged with Ankur to delay the trip. But in response, Ankur said, "No idea uncle, Chris is having the plan of execution with him, he will be reaching the Airport in some time."

Dad said, "Listen Isha, we don't have anyone in the fashion field, I have no sign or clue of how it is. I have given you the liberty to choose the career of your choice but please ensure me that you'll not be at risk."

I replied, " Sure dad, will take care. Prolly this is the silliest moment in recent times."

Prompting 'sure' then lag 'uncle' and continued, "I'm Chris who sponsored this event, please don't worry, will give all my support for her to peak her career. She has dedication towards her profession and has given her best so far."

Dad's expression was like who's this crazy guy interrupting us and retorted to him, "I know she will give her best. But how will you cater to her success through your support." (his inner voice meant like will you sponsor all my daughter's events)

Chris replied, "Uncle, just that I would be a facilitator in her career progression. She is smart, bold, impressive and highly competitive since everything is in place for her it will be a cakewalk for her to go to the next level. Well, I only modulated her to move to London for seeking a better future."

Dad immediately turned and looked into my eyes I showed irrational look. Understanding this guy will put me into trouble if I do not intervene him. So I said, "I will visit London now as a perk to my work as there are no concrete plans for sustaining the stay."

Now I thoroughly experienced how Ankur feels in his company. Placing my luggage in trolley he spoke, "It's time to leave, let's not delay."

Dad felt irritated with the voice of Chris and was shocked to see his dominance. Finally, I and dad were reciprocating missing messages while Chris mentioned to Ankur, "Isha is my only dear responsibility, rest all you keep an eye." Thank God dad didn't hear that.

Ankur replied, "Will do that, but on one condition you have to bear the entire trip covered costs."

Chris said humorously, "Hahaha!!!! Yes bro, anything for her and signalled something to him."

Both approached me with a giant smile, "Isha you are travelling separately with us (me, you and, Chris)."

I questioned back, "Why can't you include everyone?"

Chris with pride in his voice replied, "You are special from others for your awesome works."

At that moment, Ankur bent his face down to hide his expression. Apparently, my flight was cut off from the other designers, so was unaware as to how the journey went for them, and to my refinement, these guys did some breathless entertainment.

At big Mansion. Galloping through huge gateways, I delved myself into having a glimpse of the fairy land. After passing by the cascade you can view a massive castle that is beautifully engraved in detail. There are no distinctive words to describe it, you have to simply experience its charisma. For a moment, I couldn't believe my eyes that what I just saw is real and also the fact that Chris resides here. We were welcomed with high spirited joy and sanctioned our respective rooms. When I looked around, I was so thrilled to see Greek women's fluorescent paintings and was tempted to experience those ancient typical style adoptions.

Chris escorting me, spoke, "You relax now, will take you through the whole dynasty later." And continued, "Well this is my ancestral hardearned belongings and not any of my contribution. For me more than anything else, this is based on the honest belief of being self-made and I truly value him the most."

Initially, I got attracted by the pleasant natural aroma from tulip flowers that were arranged in porcelain vases and the shining brocade curtains did resist me to come out of the room. So I took my own sweet time to unwind. Half a day later, I went deep down searching for Chris and found him in the kitchenette space. He was marinating the chicken while next to him a cute chubby lady was chopping the veggies and assisting him with the required stuff. I approached them. Watching me he opened up the conversation, "Isha, is everything fine? You might be hungry, just give me some time and food will be served."

And they both searched between the cooking items. Chris to her, "When will mom be back from Jerusalem?'

She addressed him as Chri (sounds like cry), "No intimation from her end, but I do remember that it will be difficult for her and Mr. Stephen to attend the Royal wedding as there is conflict in the dates, so she instructed if you are in the city then to make it happen."

His response was, "Oh, is it? Let's see to it then."

And then he smiled to me stating, "By the way she is Loba who takes charge of our cookery section, a British chef trained in Indian foods and has a very keen knowledge of our culture & tradition. Most of the time you will find her in slack clothes.(Her expression sounded like, "Oh no, this is a bad kind of intro.")

I greeted her saying, "Very pleased to meet you Loba." She responded, "Same here dear."

And then continued, "You know, Chri is very naughty and both of us enjoy the status of being partners in crime. We are consistently successful by not getting into the notice of Mrs. Stephen."

I replied, "Really? I can't wait to hear more about what you guys do and please tell me more about Chris. Let's have some private conversation at a later point in time."

His expression was like don't do that but actually, he meant please do it. At dining, Loba displayed the food articulating on delicious combos. She sat right next to me and in my left, Chris was seated. From either side, they both were so delighted to make me relish different flavours of tastes. I was overflowing with their cordiality and this guy is beyond awesome for his amazing talks. The way he portrayed himself to all the other designers has craved their interest towards him, and they really couldn't come out of his aura. He mesmerized them with the utmost caring and grabbed their attention on how and what can be done in their week's visit. Ankur joined us late-night, seeing Loba's continental cuisine he excitingly mentioned, "Even if she'll cook crocodiles, it'll taste amazing."

Chris remarked, " By God's grace she left for the day or else would weep to hear that her tempting food was wrongly perceived to be cooked as bitter gourd shaped reptiles, and so far where did you disappear."

Ankur replied, "Was at a restaurant bar with Keme on his new business appeal, he proclaimed your portfolios are outstanding. So he is looking forward to a commercial brand from us in the coming months. Seems like he wants to associate with us."

Chris said, "Well if it is an explicit deal, can tie up but can't really commit as of now."

One of my dear colleagues confidently reacted to it. Saying, "Just focus on India. You guys are well known for your works there."

Winking to Chris, Ankur replied to her, "We don't confine our business for a particular geography." And continued, "Due to personal reasons our prime focus is on the United Kingdom now." Smiling at his response and checking my expression Chris stopped him to mention something further to us.

I couldn't escape from Chris showing my mousey smile. Noticing it he said, "How can I fail to keep my promise."

Ankur said, "Are you serious? When did you start taking oaths?"

I don't know why but an innocent response came unknowingly from me, "Actually Chris gave assurance to my dad that he will help me to peak my career."

"Wow! That's superb news."

Ankur and others hummed in the chorus 'Oh Hu ho ... oh Hu ho ho... oh Hu ho ho ho."

Then Chris tried to hide my statement to save his dignity, "She can make it by herself, just that I will be there as tiny support in her successful journey."

For the first time, I felt that I can take off my pride of independence from deep inside of me to depend on this guy for my desires. And days just passed by spending time with him on lengthy talks.

******

Preps for Royal wedding

Chris made solid efforts to convince Loba to attend the wedding along with us. She, however, reacted with a strict 'no' so he felt very despondent. There was a girly shy instinct shown by me as Chris continuously stared at my outlook. I was dressed in a peach coloured fabric gown which was one of the fabulous designs of mine. It had sparkling imprints on its open multi-layers. I had to do some random stuff consciously moving back and forth to divert his sight off from me. Oh God please divert his looks or I can't accompany him to the event.

Seeing my imbalanced moves here and there he gently held me and pleasingly checked, "Shall we go."

I replied softly, "Yes, How about Loba?"

Chris replied, "She has some inhibitions to come. I tried comforting her but failed to make her agree."

I replied to him, "Let me give one last try and attempted to persuade Loba, saying, "Hey dear, I am gonna design the best costume for you that will surely boost your confidence. Just gimme some time."

I took a black plain cloth and red velvets from the closet and used the room's brocade curtains to lay out a beautiful attire.She was so shocked when I wrapped the curtain clothing onto her body structure to make a perfect design and then alternately filled the brocade portions with red velvet and also black cloth leading to the floral gown. Due to time constraint, I had to loosely stitch some patches of the design and for firm support attached them with glue. Once it has been done I made her stand in a static position and then sometime later she excitingly checked herself in the mirror and stated, "Wow! It's a magical look, now there is no stomach bump and the belly fat disappeared completely." Her smile explained everything.

We both did a wary walk with high heels on, this time Chris was staring at Loba with a pell-mell face. He complimented after scrutinizing her, "You look too stunning. Looks like this was put on our wall screen. How did you manage to wear it on your body."

Loba was on cloud nine and she reverted to him, "This is Isha's fantastic creation and I'm in love with it. Now it's time to grace the Royal wedding."

Showing his lovely smile, uttered with the low bass tone, "I know my girl did it. "Then raised his voice to us,

"You both took a lot of time so we would be late for the wedding."

Loba then cryingly sung a song, "Wanna met you my charming prince and I know you'll be there I am coming." Sprinkling water drops all over she madly danced around the cascade.

Chris screamed, "Loba be careful. You would fall." And went running to her. By the time he reached she was supported by one of the cascade pipes that prevented her from falling. He gently took her down saying, "You're one happy lady today, women look great with their self-esteem not really by the looks. Just try to be this way."

His flow of speech was stopped suddenly when he heard a towering feminine voice asking, "Aren't you becoming late?"

He shockingly replied, "Yes mom, when did you arrive ?"

She responded, "I have come when our chef turned into Cleopatra and then I was having fun silently watching you guys while the drama was going on."

Loba's revert was so funny. She said, "Attention, please. Let us continue with this once we are back from the wedding. Now let's not make the Royal couple wait."

Chris was driving one of his favourite old blue Chevrolet Vintage Belair with beetles music on alongside his mom. He introduced me to her. She is a very good observant. Her talks were most prone to impulsive arguments. Loba signalled me on her sudden innate change in interest to check into some other celebrations and sighed on skipping the event to go for the Casino.

Mrs. Rose Stephen instantly reacted, saying "Yes you guys can have lots of fun and joyful time."

Our Chris was into his own world of music, hearing his mom's response, he gave a disheartened look to both of us that sounded like you guys please don't miss out to attend the wedding. But then with huge disappointment, he had to drop us at one of the most happening Casinos that was run by a valiant British lady. There was sizzling lavish women crowd of discrete age groups frittering money away. I was clueless where Loba headed as there were hundreds of slots of casino games. Suddenly there was a loud cheer up and appreciation from a vibrant group. "Excellent lady, you are very fortunate. Your treasure multiplied ten times." And several reactions followed, the lady valiant who is like a monster added a worrisome flavour to it, "You Indians are very smart, even a big gambler like me would lose and can get into debts. There should be a limit for you guys or else I may have to close down my casino."

Then this young smart lady returned the pounds that she earned stating, "I have come here to have fun, not really for the greed of winning oodles of cash. I actually get kick-ass fun when I lose while I spent."

Her reciprocation instigated a spirit of inquiry in me so I went close by to check. I was next to her while she announced loudly "Let us play to lose to the scratch. Then with an intriguing look, she asked me, "Indian?" .She, however, did reveal vague Indian looks.

I replied, "Yes, I am Isha from India. How about you?" I asked while shaking her lofty palms.

"Well, I am Sania, an Indian born residing in Great Britain, and running a restaurant for living. You do seem like a first-timer here." And continued to check whether anyone accompanied me.

Probing around I shockingly pointed, "I have come with her over there." Loba was performing pole acts.

Sania showed excitement, "Wow! let's make some noise with the sound clap."

Then she screamed loud to Loba, "Lady dazzler you are crazy." Then went on to do high volume clapping. She was doing terrific bold moves and checked with me excitingly if I can join her for dance. Stamping on the feet of women in the crowd, making excuses and gushing from them we managed to step up on the gaming table. With heels off, I and Sania did sway dance without a split break. Our bodies were in perfect sync to the rhythm of the high beats. There were moments when we escaped from falling while tapping our feet. The right thing we did was supporting each other with our hand moves. And this continued for hours. Lastly involving the crowd we did some contemporary form of dance that Sania liked the most. She rushed stating, "It was awesome being with you. Would like to hang out later, let's stay in touch." and we exchanged our contacts.

We were so exhausted that we started to palpate like a dog. With disbanded hair and broken heels in hand stepped out of the Casino, Loba's ultimate act led to the design patches to drop off and part of the attire was abandoned. I could imagine thinking of our appearance how pathetic we were looking now. After the wedding time, Chris waited long for us and strangely looked at us. He funnily commented, "what did you guys do inside? Did someone eat away the dress and broke the heels?" Loba was drunk and not conscious of what was happening around. She only managed to spell out Sania's name.

He stopped being hilarious and in a concerned way, asked, "Who is she?"

I replied to him, "Loba is not in her senses, not sure what is she speaking of. We just met that girl in the Casino."

Chris managed Loba to get into his car and drove fast to her home, he walked tiptoed inside the room while I followed his steps and checked with him, "Why so silent moves."

He revealed on our drive back, "Loba has a small wild lamb, she brought it from the Morgan's place."

I grieved, "Oh God, one step on it would have led to its suffering."

He replied, "Haha, I observed it was in the middle of billets in the living room."

He continued with multiple breaks on the way. Then at one time, he said, "There is a surprise for you from my end and halted at his favourite spot. It was his dad's tomb. A holy place that was more sacred to him than paying a visit to a Chapel. He mentioned, "There couldn't be any better place than this."

After spending some moments there, we went back to the Castle. While getting down from the car he mentioned, "Mom would like to talk to you tomorrow during the breakfast hours."

******

Next day

I couldn't wake up at the usual time, the next morning. It was a dragging night as I didn't have enough sleep the previous day. Had spoken to mom about Chris's love proposal and my equal feelings for him. Her determined response was, "It's not that easy to be agreed on. Your dad, granny should accord it as fine. I will suggest you not to keep any expectations."

Being perceptive I replied, "I will do it if it is a very righteous thing for me. I can make out on true bonding and best relationships. Ours can't be a worrying connection at all."

A rapid tring tring sound alerted me to check my mobile. It was Chris's message- "Don't be late."

Seeing that I hurriedly began to get ready and went down. His mom was leisurely waiting at the breakfast table, she gestured me to have a seat and spoke strongly.

"Loba isn't present today. Seems like she didn't come out of the aftermath of yesterday's celebration so I had to prepare breakfast."

I replied, "Wow that's cool. Let me try."

She mentioned, "I am a terrible cook. Long ago when Chris was eight years old, that was the last time I baked a Christmas cake."

I served myself cluttered cheesy spring noodles on my plate alongside french fries and a diet coke. Hearing her candid speaking, I dared big to taste the food. And to my shock, she mentioned, "You should be fine after having this food."

This lady is exactly how I am. Doesn't put any covering thought for whatever she feels. To an extent, she is a replica of me. Suddenly she questioned unpleasantly, "Isha you have come here from India to seek your career, so what are you up-to?"

Though it was of right eloquence, I felt offended and even annoyed but didn't think much of what to reply to her because could not make sense of what really I have to say. So shortly responded.

"I am working on it. Since an international platform is a big-time chance if you get it your way."

She reacted, "Are you expecting Chris's potential hand for this?"

I confidently replied to her, "Not really, I am trying to be a self-build person so he has to hardly get involved."

She then mentioned, "I appreciate you. Chris is just like you as he too prefers to stand on his own. He abounds to have a basic standard of living than to stay in the lap of luxury. Every time I directed him to our business he walked away responding that it is not his cup of tea."

She prolonged to say, "Last evening during the wedding he only spoke about you. It clearly showed that he likes you and not to any of my surprise expressed that he met his soulmate. Giving a smile, a rare trait of hers. She continued to mention, "So do you have the same feelings for him? And see him as a right partner for you."

I replied, "Well Rose, we are poised to passionate love and I feel both of us make great companionship. Just have to get my family's consent on our relationship."

She reverted, "You are self-reliant and so is my son, then why do you think family's intervention is needed here."

I didn't mark her words but commented on her heuristic thought, "There lies sensibilities to authentic Indian families to approve on relationships and independent living can be of zero factors to deal with their opinions and emotions."

Isha always preferred black thick cappuccino so I quietly shelved an extra pack of coffee beans for her to notice. Whereas I like to have a sugary syrup solution. I added a sugar cube to sip from the mug. Isha was enjoying tasty coffee I, however, did interrupt her by anticipation that was running in my head, 'What if Rose would have objected to your love.'

She reacted quite normally, 'Rose doesn't believe in conditioning the love. To her, a relationship is not subjective to external interference and is an absolute private affair between partners.' She continued to express.

'Chris did mention to me after his parent's divorce. Rose waited almost a decade for true love to happen and found it in Mr. Stephen who also believes the same.'

Amidst all these, I feel Chris should be rewarded with the title of the most understanding man. Isha responded in affirmative, saying, 'Yes, he is, I agree. One day what happened you know. I and Chris were in his personal bar chamber. While having the conversation about his extended families. Rose has come and asked to excuse her for disturbing our private space. I felt it be a very formal gesture of her.'

She instructed and urged me to meet one of the fashion experts that day as she took an appointment. Chris with composed tone replied to her, "Mom not sure why you are always after Isha, let her think of her own."

His mom replied, "You know whom I am referring to. It's Stella." He reverted, "So what mom?"

Giving a kind of serious look to her and checked with me, "Are you okay to meet."

Well, I didn't want to be the reason for them to get into arguments, so I did say "That's fine, will do." Then Rose asked Chris to leave us for some time. He, however, did it with some reluctance. She then mentioned to me, "As you prefer not to have his potential hand for support, here you have the scope to do it by yourself." And conveyed on the rise of Stella from an ordinary girl to one of the leading designers on the fashion streets.

After listening to it I said, "The journey of Stella is quite influential.

With all the triumphs and struggles she encountered it's unbelievable for what she is now."

She then responded, "I know and felt like telling you because you also come from a similar middle-class background. So, therefore, could relate to the struggles and gain impetus for your journey."

I don't like any discrimination based on one's family status or class. It has nothing to do with one's accomplishments. She could sense that from my rude expression. So she asked to pardon her for reacting too fundamentally. I deliberately didn't respond to her and headed off without an acknowledgment. I took the address specification. Marked the appointment time and then took my designs to travel to Stella's place which was known as 'House Of Stile Vestito'. I could reach promptly and hardly had to wait to see Stella. Her appearance was very simple. Unlike any other fashion iconic figures, she prefers casual wear and also the unusual bronze hairstreaks. I greeted her with a 'hi', she liked my style, complimented on my neck rhodium jewels and paper fabric scarf.

Her developments in fashion are truly of my interest so I have decided to take up some expert training from her. And when I expressed that to her, she took my designs to go through, selected one of them and checked if she can market my template in an event where she is the guest of honor.

I was so excited for that and said you can add some additional patterns for a better exhibit. She said this should be fine and appreciated Indian designers for their versatile fashion sense. They design conventional patterns with a modern outlook. My designs for Rose usually blend with both. And mentioned about their bonding and the relationship they share. She said, "Actually today, I am at my private time with no models and designers around. Just for her, I guaranteed your appointment."

I said, "That's so nice of you."

She then raised her eyebrow showing a sense of surprise and said, "I came to know from Rose that you and Chris are dating each other. So I wish the best romance to happen to both of you that ever happened in the history of best couples."

I was awestruck because I never thought that we should be someone idealistic to others and even set the benchmark for love. Though I did react with a smile and said, "I hope so Stella and thanks for wishing us."

She has portraits of people with torn clothes. So I curiously checked what it could be, she seemed to get emotional to talk about it, her voice expressed sudden grief.

"This is the evidence of my life lived on the streets of London with dying poverty. I never imagined my family would live with no money and be abandoned. There was a big challenge for shelter, food, clothing, and facing this every day was the biggest fear we all had. And I don't want to forget those important days of my life."

When Rose conveyed to me about the struggles faced by Stella, I could only feel for this lady but now I could see the pain of her struggle through her own eyes. I then turned to one attractive display, she was very happy to talk about it, "I was fortunate to save my mother's wedding gown that got split into pieces. I used my design techniques to complete it. I can proudly say this was my first test for designing and has its appreciation till date."

With a confidence that one day even my designs would create a sensation, I pulled myself out from her house. As I saw Chris, I strained my eyes with a piercing stare. Oh God, he is here.

He asked, "Why didn't you want me to come with you?" I replied, "Nothing like that, I never said that."

He unwrapped the scarf from my neck and asked, "Why are you wearing this paper cloth?"

I replied, "To ease your work to wipe off tears."

He pulled me close to him and politely asked, "Baby, What happened"

"Nothing just got lost in the midst of Stella's awesome work, I really should do something like her."

He said, "You will honey. And everything you want will be yours with time."

I didn't know that the little champ was there at home. He was taking rounds all over the place with kitchen grills in hand that was dismantled. So Loba had to run after him.

She grieved, "You little devil, just give up I am damn tired." Somehow Chris could hold him, "Hey champ, return the grills." Gazing at me he asked Chris, "Is she your girlfriend?"

Chris smiled, "Yes, how do you like her?"

Tony quickly replied, "Why should I like your girl?"

Chris couldn't utter anything back and released him to Loba. Giving back the stuff, the champ spoke, "If you run, you will slim down and it will be easy for you to chase me."

She showed a bright smile and put him on her lap, "Mr. Stephen is home. So let's be disciplined, we shall play all these in his absence."

For her, both stepbrothers are playful mates who like to do all kinds of notorious stuff. I don't know why but I felt like talking to my family especially with my younger cousin. So was climbing the stairs fast to dial from my room's extension.Chris spelled my name loud, "Hey why are you hurrying? I told him that I needed to relax for a while."

I couldn't connect immediately and waited for sometime to channel the signal. Dadi picked the call and spoke, "Hello beta just thinking of you? How are you?"

I was about to respond to her that I was doing good when suddenly, mom interrupted from the other room and spoke from the same connecting line "Any moves on your career path?"

I said, "Mom I got a leap, met a fashion specialist here. So I see more prospects."

She said, "Okay good." and then continued to say, "I had a word with your dad about your interest in Chris."

"Is it mom? What did he say?"

"Your dad's initial response was, 'She is there to make her trip meaningful and should work on things that advance her fashion career. And I want her to focus this.' But later having some extended discussion with all the family members he expressed, 'I met Chris at the Airport during Isha's travel, he didn't portray his actual character, cannot decide unless we spend time with him and his family. So let's invite them to India.'"

I was delighted because dad's invite was a huge achievement. When I enquired for 'Chhotu Bachha' she said he has gone out with uncle. Then I ended the phone call saying, "Mom let me put this across to Chris and inform you back."

As I took the time to go down. Chris worried something had happened. I saw him coming through the window so opened the door with smiles.

He said, "Oh Gosh! I thought you are upset." I replied, "Why would I be?"

He then armed me and asked, "Why don't you join us for some booze? Stephen has won an old dated Champagne through bidding in an auction. He had spent a million pounds on this."

I reacted, "Wow! Guess what? Dad invited all of you to visit India and come home."

He asked, "Any reason?"

"Dad knows we both like each other. So he said, Let both the families meet to discuss the matter."

Chris replied, "That is amazing, baby. Will make it for sure. Now we have something to celebrate." He winked.

That was a pretty awkward moment. Stephen rolled the Champagne bottle on the floor indicating who would be the first to grab it. Unnoticed Loba stepped on it and slid along with it that eventually made him fall on his back. Chris immediately helped Stephen to stand while Loba picked the high priced leaking bottle and asked for his forgiveness. She had to cover up the whole thing with just a simple apology. The way Stephen fell was hilarious. I madly laughed loud and it was so loud that I could see Chris disappointed look as he sighed to move away from there.

After settling down on the table he spoke, "You freaking girl, mom was upset about your behaviour.'

I told him, "What to do, couldn't resist myself."

He said, "My crazy darla!" And expressed his concern, "Loba feels awful about what happened today, let me talk to her and come."

I replied, "OK."

Not sure what Rose felt on my unexpected reaction for Stephen. She smiled and introduced me to him as Chris's girl.

Stephen said with amazement, "Surprising! he is dating an Indian girl." Rose replied, "Hmm, she is his first girl."

I couldn't make out if I have to take that as a compliment or not. I just nodded with no expression on my face. And thought, this is the right time to inform them about dad's invite to India and did tell them about that.

Rose reacted, "I say as it's a mutual liking for you both. Just don't bother about family and as you guys wish, try to plan for your marriage."

And then Stephen reacted, "Why your family should be certifying your love."

I didn't want to respond strongly. But did it because I had to make them understand how important it is, "In India, marriage is just not confined to a girl and a boy. It involves the families of both the girl and the boy equally. It's not enough, even if both of them like each other. The boy's parents should like the girl and girl's parents should like the boy and only then, the marriage will take place."

Stephen gave a heavy expression, "Looks like marriage in India is a method and a well-followed procedure."

I gave them a sober response, "Marriage is neither a method nor a procedure, it is just one's belief on how to address it."

They acknowledged my feelings and said, "We shall meet your family. You can inform them."

Sometimes you have to put extra efforts to simply convey your opinion. Just imagine if you are in a position to make them agree to do something. I got this sense of challenge while the conversation was happening with Mr. and Mrs. Stephen. I wondered if I was over speaking because all these are not subjects of my age. Whatever at least I was able to convince them.

Chris played some romantic melody songs that turned out to be the perfect music for the couple to dance. Rose took the lead and did strange moves holding Stephen. I could relate that to Loba's dance at the Casino. Chris was so shocked to see his mom crawling up to Stephen and doing strange moves. Loba's mood was all set now. She asked Chris if he can come for a couple dance. Stephen's pair gave way to them and encouraged them by clapping. Chris offered his hand to Loba and without bothering anyone around they both did some terrific moves. Suddenly, I saw blood imprints on the floor.

I yelled, "Loba stop! You are bleeding."

She didn't bother to hear so had to stop their dance. Then Chris even noticed it and said to her, "How did you fail to see there are glass granules on the floor that pierced through your stockings."

Loba panicked, "Oh God! I'm shedding blood."

I wondered to myself, "Why didn't she realize it, is there no pain to her?"

Rose and Stephen had to surge to attend sacred prayers, they said to Loba to take care and left. I and Chris wandered for the first aid kit. He was the first to get it, then quickly removed the glass pricks and did dressing.

"Hey, what's up!" a surprise text from Sania.

I immediately could get who it was as I had saved her contact as "Sania UK."

I replied, "Just in a small party, too close to home. What's up with you."

She then responded, "Oh is it?" And in continuation message, she wrote, "Today is our restaurant's anniversary. So giving an offer for everyone to have unlimited cocktails. If you are interested then you can walk-in along with your friends and avail it."

That moment Loba's face brightened like a twinkling star. She went damn crazy on reading it and said I would love to go. Chris however, was reluctant to take her request because of her condition.

He looked at me and asked, "Baby who is it?" I said, "She is that Casino girl."

He said, "Okay. What did you say?"

I mentioned, "I don't have any problem if Loba's doesn't." He replied, "I can do that."

Well, I felt that as a friend and as a true companion, he is the one to bond with. The way he was taking care of Loba was evidence of that. As we were approaching the destination point, he said to me, "This is the bar where Ankur usually hangs out. This is the most happening place for him."

I was very surprised to know that. The minute we entered the place, Sania looked at Loba and remarked, "You will be one happy person today, you can have as much as you want. But unfortunately, there are no poles." She smirked.

Loba expressed her inability and said, "Not in a position to do any of those acts or dance today."

Sania laughed. "Who is responsible? Is that you, rolling her eyes to him."

Loba said, "You have to excuse yourself for your talks, he doesn't trouble people even for fun."

Sania, "Sorry gentleman. Hope you will pardon me."

Chris reacted to them with a 'lol' expression. I occupied one of the corners, next to the fireplace to get the warmth. The whole arrangement was very interesting. The roof above has hanging digitals 9to1 on which remarkable achievements for that particular year was shown.

There were pictures of restaurant crews with happy faces and also some privileged customers put as flash exhibits. I could easily trace out Ankur from a set of noticeable group flashes. Sania came away from providing service to customers, "These are high numbered clients so I had to put on my serving dungarees to address them." And questioned me with concern "Why are you here? There are big pitchers right in front. You can drink as much as you want you from those."

I replied, "Am not a much of an alcohol loving person."

She smiled and said, "Though I run a bar I don't prefer to have it myself as well. But today, I want you to taste something special."

We went to the beverage serving area, signalling the tapster she took two different drinks, mixed both in same proportion and just by adding ice cubes she offered me a glass and said, "You will love it"

I wondered if it was so simple to make and while sipping the drink, was surprised by the taste as the taste was equivalent as raspberry fruit. I also told her the same.

She replied, "I know it." And looked around to offer Loba the drink aswell.

Chris denied her drink and remarked, "I think it's a bad idea. She is already into overtaking."

Sania didn't force her and politely checked with me, "How do you know Chris?"

I said, "I am a fashion designer by profession, he sponsored serial events of mine that happened in India. Through him, my journey to London has started."

She gave a shocking expression, "Oh god! You design clothes, smartest and difficult work."

And mentioned, "I thought you and Loba are friends and Chris is someone in common to you both."

I replied, "Loba is a chef in his home. But she is more like a family to them."

She reacted, "Awww that's really nice." Then she took a broad view of my attire and asked, "Did you design this love?"

I said, "No. This isn't one of mine. But mine is pretty similar." She exclaimed, "Ahh! you still look fab in this."

Chris intervened our conversation and said, "Sorry to break this, but ladies we should depart now, cannot handle Loba anymore."

I felt he behaved like a barrier to her freedom and I somehow didn't like his attention towards her.

Sania exclaimed, "What's this dude? You guys didn't even start celebrating. At least have a dance?"

I said, "When it comes to dancing, I can never say no."

Sania reacted, "Of course! I know that. I can't stop myself from complimenting you from the time of your dance at the casino. You were such a hot babe."

Chris, "Yes she is."

Then he immediately took me off onto the dance floor. I asked Chris

looking into his eyes, "Am I your first love?"

He said, "Yes, dear." Then I asked one more question.

"Am I your first partner in a dance."

He smiled and confessed, "You are not! But you will remain as the last one with whom I will ever dance."

He was too fast in turning me around, so quick in shifting me to his left and right. I only did some troubling moves and couldn't do any steps syncing with his. I don't know what happened but he did a damn comfortable dance while I did not. However, it was Sania who enjoyed our dance thoroughly jumping on her toes. She screeched in such a way that even the glass pitchers trembled. I liked her chilled out actions. Loba was completely shut down and was on the verge of losing consciousness, sloping directionless here and there. Sania saw that and ran and gave support to her to lean on. But she couldn't manage Loba's big physical structure. She then called our names aloud to help her, so our crazy performance was called off.

Chris remarked, "Shit man! she puked." I said like a little munchkin.

"See her changing pink face."

Chris said, "Loba. Don't lose your balance. Hold me and let's go." She didn't move, so he lifted her and made her sit in the car saying, "You are on the couch." I could get a strange smell from him. His shoulder and arms were completely wet in alcohol. He seemed like he had alcohol all over him.

Sania said with concern, "Guys. Get home safe. Well, manage yourselves and let me know if you need anything."

Chris said to me, "Loba is crippled both physically and mentally, can't take her home in this state so let her be with you tonight."

******

It was late India in India when I telephoned mom. Accidentally, dad also attended the call. I was so happy that I got a chance to speak to him. I announced without a pause, "Dad listen. Chris and his family are coming to India."

He replied, "OK! let them come on the day of Chotu's thread ceremony."

Suddenly Chris talked with a high pitched voice, "She is moaning. Just take care of her."

I was surprised to hear his voice and said, "You still here." Dad asked, "Who's that you are talking to."

I said, "It is Chris."

Dad reacted, "To whom he is referring."

I said, "We had been to a restaurant anniversary. Our common friend Loba was high on alcohol. She is there with me now."

Dad remarked, "Don't be adaptive to an unrealistic lifestyle. I heard from mom you are staying at Chris' home. Why don't you live on your own?"

I replied, "Hold on dad." And sighed to Chris, "Don't worry! Will keep an eye on her. You can leave." And then with a tone of confidence continued to speak on the difficulty to get a home to stay.

He listened with utmost understanding whatever I conveyed, though reasonable he still repeated to take his ideal believe to my head. Dadi was actively following his conversation so she took gadget from him and said, "Beta tu ghabara mat, ghar dhundh lo, mujhe maloom hai, difficulty of getting home."

And she convinced him, "Usko Chris ke house mein rehne do. London ka cheez alag hai. Let her settle."

I heard her lastly saying, "She is independent enough to make her own decisions. Let her fly high. Don't chip her wings because of our insecurities." and winded the call.

Dadi always felt that I was born to achieve something big. My dad was very protective of me while she was concerned about my freedom. I thank God for having such a family. I wonder what I would do without family. I didn't drink much and also nothing went wrong with me, but my head was dropping off. Whatever be the reason I have decided to take a nap. A proper undisturbed sleep.

Immediately the next day, Sania did morning disturbance through her phone rings. Her voice seemed concerned, "Hey all good? How you guys are feeling?"

I replied rubbing my eyes that everything is fine and rolling beside didn't find Loba. So mentioned that she might have already set for a brand new day.

And remembered dad's words, so have put across the matter to Sania and asked her to find me a house to rent.

She said, "Is it? That's cool. There is an apartment nearby to my house.

I know one girl there looking for a flatmate and it's a sharing one."

I completely get dead to the world when I slept and that is my nature of sleep. Now I could hear some familiar voice talking to Chris. So with curiousness, I told Sania, "Will call you later."

And have come out to check, it was Ankur having a conversation on his global tour.

Chris hugged me, "Good Morning baby."

Ankur reacted as a dear crony and said, "I know your relationship status."

Chris replied, "Do not assume anything bro, you had been to exploring the entire planet."

He grieved, "Aww! But I could only cover the Middle East part, now you don't assume anymore."

I reacted with hearty laughter.

"By the way how is Loba?", asked Ankur.

Chris replied, "Last night you said you will keep a watch on her. but where were your eyes? I had to drop her in the dark."

I reacted, "Oh! I didn't know that.'

Chris smirked and said, "I am happy that you did keep your words." Ankur remarked, "Don't be sarcastic. She will get offended."

I replied, "Why? I am open to wisecracks." Chris remarked, "really?"

Ankur replied by mimicking my voice and said, "Of course!"

I replied, "Hello you are looking like a big clown on the screens."

Ankur replied, "When did I get on to that, didn't appear physically in recent shows. Our event in India was the last. Then after, had no money to do anymore event."

I continued saying, "Hey listen the flash photos of yours are the super stupid ones." And demonstrated fake expressions to make him feel annoyed.

Chris reacted, "You still show cuteness dear. Let me show his erratic expressions." And added that's the reason Sania's sales scaled up drastically this year and told Ankur, "You should feel like a proud man." Ankur with a pale face replied, "Sania! Who's this girl?"

It was a windy day due to severe fog happening. To overcome that I drove as fast as I can to meet Sania at the restaurant, she was at home so gave me the directions to come two miles ahead on the sideline path till I could see a public park and then to take the crossways to reach her house. I did as per the instructions that were given. As soon as I reached, I could hear people having some peculiar conversation. One is surely Sania's voice. A middle-aged man with Indian features was coming out from the entry door, observing me he buzzed Sania.

Her response to him was, "She is my friend." And told him something in her paternal language. I could only understand my name. His humble reply to her sounded like okay.

Sania said to me, "Please step in. Actually, was prioritizing some important stuff for the day. Just need some time and it has been notified that we would be coming to visit the flat."

I replied, "Sure."

In the meantime, till the time she came. I examined her living room, It was decently kept and well organized, similar to her restaurant pattern. I saw a beautiful picture of a pretty Irish lady along with a handsome Indian guy, they both looked super stunning. I was so tempted to see the picture in person.

I asked her once she was back, "Hey can I meet this beautiful couple."

She responded, "I guess you were not able to recognize him. He is my dad who was leaving while you came and she is my mom. None of us will be able to see her physically anymore."

I immediately reacted, "I am very sorry."

She replied, "No worries." And continued saying, "Mom always had a loving smile which I like to carry on with me. Her understanding of life was to live to most of what was happening because she believed life could happen just once. I truly admire what she was."

I replied, "That's beautiful. Now I understand why you are this way." She then emotionally continued, "Her smile and presence would be an impossible visual. I exist because of her but she is not with us because of our financial inability to save her. But after we lost her, our treasure multiplied rapidly. Though there are needs to be met, I don't like if money grows. I exhaust it either by hook or crook and it is not a big deal. Well, there is no point in having so much money now. Sometimes I try hard to lose the earnings and at other times it goes off easily. To be frank when I needed money it was not there but when I do not care about it anymore, it has come in a huge number."

I hugged her and said, "You are one of the strongest people I have ever met. The smiles you show and the good vibes you spread has a philosophy behind them."

It was shocking when an Indian brown-skinned girl unlatched the door, the house was full of smoke spread all over the place and smell of cigar. We two were badly coughing and I even couldn't get a clear picture of the lady.

Without a split lag, I reacted," Can you let this smoke go." She replied, "Don't worry. This is just for today."

Sania reacted, "What do you mean?"

Rizhana replied, "You know the time I broke up with Jane, I had my grey shades of life and became addicted to all these drugs and smoking. After a long gap, we have patched up again on the same unfold truth that separated us. So celebrating it by burning cigars."

I reacted, "Then are you quitting?"

Rizhana said, "Yes, not anymore. No more ill behaviour. I was depressed from being alone and did undergo a suicidal phase. I was very sad for so many reasons. Now to cover up that with bliss will be having you as my new-mate."

I smiled at her last sentence and asked, "Where is she now?"

Isha replied, "Her boyfriend is from Sri Lanka, They both had been to his homeland. On a perfect timeline vacation."

She then continued. That disturbing day, I didn't know how to convey to Chris that I would be shifting to another place, a simple move that will make dad very happy while making Chris sad. Of late, somehow informed him. While I started to pack my stuff. He was undoing it. I quickly dumped all the stuff but then he again iterated to unpack and said "You are not going anywhere."

For the first time, he didn't let me say a word. He said, "Having a random conversation in a short time cannot decide if you can stay with a person. It applies even when you are moving in with a new roommate." He sounded like dad.

Slowly placing my hands on his heart he said, "I will come here every morning just for you baby. I see you and then start my day. It could sound silly but you should know it keeps me so alive."

I took off my hands from him and said, "This is required. Please do understand."

His face has become like a hotpot at my response. But then he took an instant deep breath to gain composure and with melting emotions, he said, "I am gonna miss you."

I still remember that moment's impression of his expression.It's the most willing move but I don't know how did I overlook his feelings. And more emotional sensitiveness added with Loba. She stood like a strong pillar with tears in her eyes not allowing me to move an inch. I gave a thought to stay back and was about to express my feelings. But Chris said, "Loba let her leave, and don't even try to stop her."

I know I made two people feel very bad. I did feel very angry when he asked me, "Should I come along to drop as you can no longer live here."

That time I couldn't stop myself from breaking down. He reacted looking into my saddened visage, "Where is your scarf?" He asked, "You know that paper dressing will be useful now."

I said, "You are there instead."

He hugged me tight and said, "Your wish is to go and I don't want to miss you, my love, so you can expect my presence there."

I asked, "Every day?"

He rubbed my palms and stroked my face with his thumb wiping off

the tears and said, "Yes, I will."

Loba suddenly said, "I should tell you something about Chris. Last night he was talking to his secret friend. You should know about her?"

I got curious. I saw him he was silent so had to question him, "Who's that girl."

He didn't answer and said, "This pile up needs to be shifted before the light fades."

I said, "Hello, look at me. You didn't reply? Tell me."

Again he did let it go and announced, "Loba, I am leaving and will probably see you at dusk."

And said to me, "I will drop you and please take care."

So what I heard from Loba might be the truth and with a very bad gesture, I replied.

"You decided to ignore me without considering my feelings and emotions."

He slowly revealed, "There is one energetic woman who nurtured her grandkids by her old wisdom. She wants them to fly on their own and be independent." And has shown me old nanny's photo that was saved as a contact.

I exclaimed, "Dadi." And repeated, "My dadi, What did she speak to you about?"

He smiled and replied, "She doesn't want us to stay apart and was worried."

At my new flat, that's a fanatic reception. Two mighty girls dressed up like panther did so much of amusement. A clap and leg tap lineup by them created the perfect rhythm. I was overwhelmed by the welcome and was so surprised to know that Chris, the master of love had planned this. Sania did a cosmopolitan set up and there were sophisticated drinks for the evening. Rizhana spoke hell lot of stuff about Jane, most of it was naked truth. She is very bold yet possesses warmth and understanding. My hard work was taken care of with utmost care she filled my designer clothes in the wardrobe and also gave me the preference to occupy extra wall to wall closet. It could very well be seen that it is not having equal sharing and was more than half of both sharing space for me in the home.

Actually, Chris & I wanted to travel together to India one month before the occasion. Later at the time of the ceremony, his family would come. But one day suddenly he said, "Rose and Stephen would be visiting for the first time to India so I will come along with them."

With that disappointment from him, I travelled to Mumbai. I entered my room at a very low pace, the oil paintings on my wall were faded out and dull. Dressing room area was very dusty and for an instance cuddling pooh(teddy) looked so aggressive. I screamed, "Maa, I feel it's been too long you kept my room clean and after my last visit to home no one stepped here."

"Helllloo" with a striking pitch from the living room, someone said, "In a day your mom's idle time is hardly a few hours." And the voice echoed.

I replied, "Dad, your shout is pointless while everything over here is dirty and rugged."

Soon he has come to me and said, "Just watch it. You have a severe jiggered sight at every corner of your room. My words are not pointless. You are mean."

'I was frustrated for little things and sometimes for no reason. Those four weeks without him was hell. I called you Sonu to tell about Chris but you were also stuck with Raj's first meeting and then its after- effects.'

'Thanum thandum thananuntam was the loud voice of the day. There was music orchestra tabla, sehnayi instruments sound heard the entire day. The customs and traditions of thread ceremony were rightly followed. Chotu was looking like a groom with holy thread and sandalwood. I kissed on his cheeks expressing my love for him. No matter how much old he becomes, we will still call him Chotu as he is the youngest of all in the family.

I was into difficulty with a Kanjeevaram saree which dadi chose for me. I couldn't come soon because of the consciousness of the saree drape and there were none to assist me in settling it as all the aunts were busy with the rituals that were happening. I somehow managed to wear, "I hope it doesn't fall." I thought to myself. I arrived late to the Mantap hall where Agnihomam was proceeding. Dubai Mausi threw comments, "How strange it is? She is a lady with modern instincts and proficient fashion personality but struggling with a simple Indian saree?" And then she had put the most treasured golden necklace of goddess Laxmi onto my neck saying, "Abhi poori hogayi."

Soon Chris saw me, and he rushed towards me with romantic pep and said, "God! You are looking so gorgeous. my heart skipped a beat seeing you pretty. I am short of words to express the way you look in this beautiful saree. I haven't seen you before in this traditional outfit else would have fallen in love with you more and more."

I behaved like a complaining female, "I am glad you liked but you men should know the trouble in carrying this."

Mausi reacted to him, "She took almost three hours to appear this way." He said, "Isha is 100%, Indian woman."

I asked him, "Where are the Stephen couple?" He replied, "They are in talks with your family." I said, "Chalo let's go." And Mausi followed us.

Chris's parents were offered mithai and khakhra made by dadi but the couple absolutely denied stating, "We don't have this kinda stuff." But Chris tasted them and appreciated dadi, "Mujhe yeh taste pasand hai."

Mom was very happy and did voice out, "Chris can speak Hindi."

Chris replied, "Yes aunty, I learnt it from Isha here and there that helps my communication in India."

Kids rattled with whistling voices that scared Tony. So Rose placed him in a chair next to Stephen and said, "This is India you will listen to some noises." And mentioned to us, "He is not like Chris who is experienced and has been with the Indian community."

Then Dubai Mausi proudly expressed to Chris, "Listen our kids are too much hyper. Music is there in their blood, even their shouts and screams sound like a musical note."

He replied, "I agree, have such experiences with Isha many times." "Is it so?" I have shown him one smirk smile. And then was going through my mobile call records, when saw missed calls of Stella so dropped her a message. She immediately responded, "You have got a chance to showcase your designs at the Cavos for an international brand."

I jumped reading the text and showed it to dad. He patted my cheek and said good luck beta. Knowing this Mom also was on cloud nine, wanna share with my darling Dadi. She was trying to comfort Tony with her Indo-English ascent who was grumbling. Her focus was into setting the British kid.

Rose expressed, "Please leave him. He wants some private space which lacks here." Dadi acknowledged her with fair expression.

Mausi suddenly with an anxious face asked Rose, "How old is the little one? There seems a huge age gap between the siblings."

Rose replied, "Five years ago our little love was born. Not just the age difference, they both are very different in other manners as well. Tony replicates my dear partner Stephen whereas Chris has traits of his biological father."

There started prying whisper between all of them that Stephen is Chris's step father.

Mom covered it by saying, "You couple is dedicated to the raising of two wonderful sons."

Rose replied, "We don't believe in any specific pattern of parenting, just left them to grow at their own pace."

A sharp voice to mom said, "To her bringing up children is as similar as leaving street animals to grow'."

I heard what Mausi uttered, so wanted to end this before getting into conflicting talks. I immediately displayed some of my kathak dance performance photos to the couple. Rose didn't show much interest as did her hubby.

Stephen said, "You look so different in this dance costume." Dad replied, "Yes, because of the prosthetics used."

Dubai Mausi seemed super curious about the couple's affair. So she interrupted dad and asked Stephen, "I would like to know when did you first see Rose."

Stephen laughed like a thunderstorm at mausi's question and replied, "On a formal occasion during a business meeting. She was wearing a black mini Bodycon dress."

Not to breach their privacy I told Mausi not to ask for any more details. But she ignored me and continued to ask them, "Any filmy type scene happened like love at first sight."

Stephen replied, "No that didn't happen, we were good friends initially and dated almost two years till Tony happened."

Indian Mausi's are very smart, not sure how she sensed this, asked him upright, "So your second son was born before the wedlock."

Rose was irritated at Mausi's questioning to her husband, so she reacted, "You are right, during wedding time I was pregnant. In fact, got married with baby bump."

Mausi zipped her mouth and didn't speak anything furthermore, but mom asked Rose, "What do you understand about marriage."

Rose continued, "A relationship starts with love and should end with love. So the marriage can be an option as the true purpose is love between the two souls. If partners who are in love should not feel their love for each other, then there is no point of them being together just for the sake of marriage." And she extended further to explain, "What if Isha doesn't feel Chris's love anymore and how can they be confident that their relationship will last forever. They may find someone in years to a new bond. So like I and Stephen are with."

Once they left, Mausi showed a relieved face and remarked, "This London family is complicated. There are still a few confusions that are unchecked. But somewhere I feel Isha and Chris make a compatible pair."

Dadi said, "Yes they do." While mom showed neutral expression.

Throughout the entire discussion, Dad was a silent observant having rare interaction and I was not sure what was running in his mind. After having strong coffee in the evening he was sitting in the balcony praying to God and I was there waiting for his prayer to finish. When he opened his eyes, the first sentence he spoke was, "I know the reason why you are here? Your dad may sound stupid to you but tell me what is it that you like about Chris?"

I said, "Dad, he is more like you. Very protective and caring."

His explanation on my choice, "Strange, my daughter is very independent but needs someone who shields her with care. Not bad. You remind me of your mom, probably every woman looks for this. Let me tell you she was just 18 years old when I got married to her. She didn't expect anything from me except for being a caring husband. Initially, she thought I would be the only one on whom she has her complete right. Slowly when this family became close to her and once she started owning it, she became greedy to have extra care and support from these people and she was able to get it. As the years went by, she didn't look for only my love and care since she was getting more care, support, love, and affection that was given to her by our family. You should understand one thing that if your partner fails in his promise then the family will make you feel confident that they are there to back you. We both never feared to live together forever or even being distanced apart because of the belief in the oath taken during the marriage that we promised to obey as long as we live. That sometimes does force each other to stick to the sacred bond and there is nothing wrong in it. If you listen to Rose, I don't understand this how can you recommend if the love for each other is diminishing let's find some other person in individual lives.

Well her intentions are pragmatic. As a matter of fact, you tend to be independent in a relationship rather to commit. I have invited Chris's family to know him better through them but firstly his stepfather and mother need to be understanding about conventional relationships. As our traditional values explain, they should sync with the family and be like us. A big complication is that they don't intervene much in Chris's personal stuff while they are open on his choice saying that it is his freedom and also his right. As per Rose's ideology if she finds someone else like Stephen, do you think there won't be any kind of similar thing happening?"

I replied, "Dad, I don't have an answer for all this. I fell in love with my career. It showed me the right way to grow and to meet the right guy. He is my love. He is my strength. He is everything to me."

He said, "Beta your career started through him and that is what is exciting you, but the personal journey will not."

I reacted, "Dad, how can you say that. You are just carrying Rose and Stephen's believes on Chris."

He reacted, "I don't deny the fact that Chris is a nice guy, his persona of being loved by others has put him on top but this alone will never be fine. He should have a proper family to support you both. So I say it's a clear 'no' to your relationship and my no would be a no forever."

When dad said this with strong voice tears started dropping from my eyes but that didn't bother him. Though I am self-centric I never disobeyed his opinions. If I want something I would convince him in the best way possible and once I hear "yes" I move ahead and if I need something badly, I do wait for his yes.

I neglected myself on everything, though there were people around me. I didn't involve myself with them. Didn't know why I have become so weak that I have cried a lot un showing me. I have isolated myself from the world and didn't feel like sharing my emotions with anyone. I cut off contact with Chris without telling him the reason. He didn't know what was happening with me.

Mom couldn't see me that way, "She said we are not fine with Chris but happy to see you grow in your career. Why don't you take up Stella's offering as a challenge and do what you are capable of doing?"

That time I smiled because that way I will get an opportunity to see Chris. After all, he is the love of my life."

I spread laughter and spoke to everyone and they thought I was normal.

That was the time when I called you and invited you to my event.'

Through the grievance, immensely disheartened to Isha's forced hatred feelings for Chris that are crooked from intense love. She has deeply suppressed the feelings for him. We were in a loggia holding coffee mugs as were dehydrated the whole night and sensed it was the time Sania arrived. She loomed from mist up and greeted us with fullon energy, 'Good morning hot chics. Huh, I don't hear any response?' She then leaped on us touching our bodies before I presume you both are no more at least shake your boots. Immediately Isha tilted the coffee mug on to her.

Sania screamed, 'Are you dead! or woke up from the grave. I like caffeine in the mouth, not on the body.' and calmed down slowly while not even a drop dripped.

Isha replied, 'Yes babe. Your hollering can awaken people from their deaths. Another time, I go back to graveyard let's spend some time with each other.'

Sania intervened with guilt, 'Enough! Isha. I've already over spoken. Now you please don't continue.'

Isha replied, 'Heyyy! I didn't mean it in extreme sense. You don't have to feel so much remorse.'

And then she urged, 'Gear up buddies! Just received a text from Morgan checking if we are on the way. So let's not spend leisure time here anymore.'

Sania hurried while the door rang multiple times, 'It is Chris standingwith the car key in hand.'

Isha rushed to him, 'Sorry Chris, I had to abandon the vehicle since it was conked out.'

He responded with composure, 'You don't have to be sorry, seeing the condition of the car I can understand the severe trouble it has given to you guys. And I'm very glad my old priceless obstinate car has run till now and continues to function and though it means a lot to me. One day or the other it has to fade away. Now repair work is done, so you guys can travel.'

Later they both mimed something and then Chris left saying, 'I'm going to the airport to receive your friend.'

We started our journey, and while travelling Sania checked as to why did Chris call the car a 'priceless obstinate?'

Isha laughed and mentioned, 'This is his granny's premium car that was used way back in 60's. She is very stubborn, so he often calls it that way. And to him, lot of memories are attached to it.

He gifted me the car at his dad's burial chamber and proposed' 'This couldn't be better than anything.

I'm giving my form of love to you, please hold and reciprocate.'

Sania questioned Isha, 'Did you reciprocate your love for him?'

She responded, 'Yes, he has given his priceless obstinate to me so that I stay stubborn to him.

Before any comment on Isha's response. I rolled my eyes to Sania and spoke in a low tone, 'Don't prolong and drag this any further.'

Sania acknowledged it and diverted on Isha's fast driving and said, 'His granny would be watching from heaven, make sure nothing happens to her precious machine.'

Isha replied 'Listen, guys, because of my fast stride have reached our destination soon.'

We passed through shadow trees to range Morgan's stay, the spot can be identified through outlined meadows and thick railings around. It's a strongly built wooden house supported with bamboos. At the entrance, there is a dark room where meat is stored for animals. As we go inside scary wild roaring's can be heard.

Mr. & Mrs. Morgan always wear a holistic smile on their faces. They are calm, composed and absolutely cool partners. Just imagine them living with wild animals showing unconditional love and ensuring their protection. I was so startled when Morgan made a jaguar to stand on two legs relaxing its body on him. Isha neared to fodder it and unexpectedly started vaulting along with its little cubs. She turned out to baby playing with small ones. With strange dread & exhilaration, I asked Sania to be my borderline. Noticing me Mrs. Morgan expounded, 'Don't be scared of our Pluto (jaguar), we found it in Brazil's Atlantic forest when it was only a 3 month's old cub. You know it is most sensitive to everything that we do and has deeper emotions than us.'

Just another beautiful form of existence and she took me over. Fear in line and tightly holding Mrs. Morgan's arms I stood in front of an enormous wild, though half-closed eyes that have large black rosettes on its body. That's a deadly moment when my hand touched golden brown fur and my anxiety multiplied.

Hurray! We heard huge screams from the other side of the fence, everyone rushed to check except me and Morgan. He probed to me 'Looks like you didn't have fun with the little ones and shifted two cubs to my hand.'

Suddenly was surrounded by 6 cubs and I made a shrill scream as they tickled me.

I heard a familiar voice from behind, 'To your joy here goes one more' and placed a cub on my head. A sudden thrill of excitement and fear rushed my veins but before I managed to hold the third one I could feel a warm hug and a muscular palm holding my tender ones. I am awestruck and pulled myself away screaming 'Oh nooo.' and turned back. He threw a smile saying, 'Baby I'm here with you, don't panic. They are just cute pups like you and will not do any harm.'

Sighting Raj, I became dumbfounded trying to believe my senses. Then, with a sarcastic flavour I asked him, 'This is monsoon season and isn't your time for all those exotic island visits' followed by a broad smile.

Looking into my eyes, he said, 'I found something far more beautiful than all those and I don't want to miss u for anything.'

Isha intervened him 'Are you serious Raj? You mentioned that you are coming here for my fashion event.'

'Hey will say it openly. I haven't come for that.' he replied. And he checked my expression.

I asked him 'How you know my best friend?'

His reply was, 'She is your best friend so I made her my friend too."

Chris informed Morgan saying Raj would stay here tonight along with us. We had arranged two tents if in case one more is required carried one extra that I handed to him. He then tried to bully, 'These are not soundproof, so hearing animal loud sound doesn't scare us while inside?'

I replied with an angry face 'No, why will I?'

He pacified, 'Actually, your fear has overpowered my gut spirits and I feel it, to be so good. Didn't know about real 'fear' till I saw that in you. It's so adorable when you show that emotion.'

I said 'For your pleasure or entertainment please don't intentionally scare me. God! It's so unbearable and I never find it nice.'

He showed a promising smile and enquired the couple what is the most challenging thing in this place? they said for an uncommon person spending one night here is the biggest dare. Morgan interestingly said there is a haunted place at the nearby countryside where people heard of some ghost's presence. We go by walk almost every day but never faced any fearful spirit.

Looking at me he said, 'Then no issues of exploring it, let's have a casual walk. Except me, all were superfine with half-interest I followed them. Isha was in front line heading all of us, to her immediate back was Chris and then Sania. And I was the last but one.

Raj suddenly said, 'Ikya take a left diversion as per the Morgan's protocol.'

I reacted 'Ikya?'

He said, 'ya' what happened?'

He didn't realize that he mispronounced Isha's name.But then, 'Oh sorry she is a different girl. I asked him you know Ikya?'

He said, 'Yes I know her and also the lady Tyson episode.' I was surprised and asked, 'How come?'

He then replied, 'Exactly one of my cousin's friend is Ikya who knows you fondly. We all happened to meet at one celebration and have become close. During normal talks, she spoke about her friends, specifically about you. And while showing her most partying clips have seen a video of yours, I liked you at first look so willingly checked about you. Though she didn't reveal much I somehow got to know the details.

Is it? She never mentioned this to me.

He reacted 'She was very casually explaining her lifestyle, friends, and stuff that intrigued me. She might have not thought that I would show interest in you and carry the matter further.'

Oh God!!! this is shocking. And he continued, 'The other day poor Ikya was waiting at the pub, just to receive me. I was supposed to come for you but didn't as your dad seemed very conventional that might have led you into troubles. He emphasized plenty of times that my son would accompany my daughter while you meet. As a consequence, my job had become more to impress two people. And by the way, though ours is like meeting strangers, the background behind was that I fell in love with you at the very first sight, and don't judge me how it happened. I was craving to see you had waited long for 4 months. So have spoken to my parents that I am interested in this girl. Then they have approached your parents as an alliance. But I have done my homework in and out about you. Technically, that was my first date with the girl I am in love.'

I was in utter shock and didn't know how to react. I said I couldn't believe it. It means you know me before we met each other. Isha heard him and reacted, 'Mujhe bhi yeh cheez shocking hai. I thought he had shown interest post the date.'

He then revealed something, 'I like to bloat my body in the air, and as higher the altitude the stronger it excites me. My buck up adventure so far was free fall from 9000 feet. I was so thrilled while hanging horizontally with my posture being parallel to the earth. It gave me the adrenaline rush but the sweet feeling of you has dominated that.'

I was nostalgic when he mentioned this to me. I don't believe in first love/first meet but this man has changed everything of that. Sania couldn't escape by the time Isha alarmed there is a pit for the animal trap. She was in a black dress and got immersed deep inside the pit that was covered by dry leaves and broken branches. We could only see the sparkling eyes of hers and was so stunned at her sudden fall that we were just looking at her doing nothing. Chris removing the stuff on her gave his hand 'These sharp twigs are unique, let's collect them.'

Sania said, 'Hello guys, what is more, important than me. Why you people are motionless and stuck in one place?'

Raj said, 'Don't turn back. Behind you, there is one and he stopped.'

I screamed as loud as I could. All of them laughed and that irritated me.

I then didn't speak anything and walked front, they also said let's go. Raj added, 'Though didn't experience the phantom at least heard haunting scream from Sonu's voice.'

By the time we went, the couple displayed wine decanters and with overflowing humbleness offered us a variety of stodge foods. They made barbeques with different animal meat. How could one deny something that was served with love but I had to do so. I didn't want to eat it so went away to search for the eatables that mom packed exclusively for Isha while travelling from India.

'Hey, Sonu come here. No need to look for food. This is the food that you like, your favourite food is being made. He has put some additional spices before it was given to me. Have it, baby.'

He was chuckling at me the way I had, without leaving the smallest of small pieces, I emptied the plate. It was so yummy but didn't feel like complimenting him.

We were tired after the days spent at Morgan's house. Time has come to leave with memories to cherish. An energetic announcement from Raj 'Guy's, let's do some race (girls vs. boys).' With drooping posture, Sania reacted. But our vintage has some trouble starting. He smartly said, 'Go with over pace while driving it. You shouldn't be a spoilsport and have to have the game spirits to win.'

Isha responded, 'Are we fools? You guys have such a sophisticated speedy one and how can you expect us to compete with this old engine. Just fairly say us to be losers.'

Chris said, 'You can exchange with the Jaguar.'

Then Isha replied, 'This should be fine. We geared up like power- packed girls.'

While we got into the car she mentioned this intensified fragrance is Rose's perfume so we may smell like her in some time. Sania laughed and said the countdown has already begun 3...2....1. These crazy guys are planning to take some unknown faster route to reach the finishing point first.

Chalo, Sonu let us take this direction to beat them. We travelled through the trodden path. There was no clear view as the black mist was coming towards us and no smooth go as the road has hard crushed paw impression. I was terrified sitting in the driving seat as we had no clue whether we were heading in the right direction Just parallel to us we heard some screaming from woods so two bravos asked me to stop the vehicle to check what it is, while they were about to open the car door a tiger leaped onto the vehicle top it missed to attack us in a fraction of second. The animal did big roaring and started to shake the vehicle.

I become motionless, with fear I started to sweat, by the jerk of the machine both came forward from their seats and fell on my body. They could feel my body has got so cold, in that tremendous physical body moment Isha searched for mobile quickly and could call Morgan with heavy palpitation. She spoke that we got stuck in dark woods under threat from a predator and was just trying to save ourselves. And suddenly the phone slipped. Then it became more scaring while the wild animal did stampede, due to cracking a rough hole was formed and one of the animal's paw could reach Sania's hair surface. She boldly pricked the animal with the twigs that were placed in the car and irritated it to calm down. She said, 'Just imagine if it completely breaks, we all are gone.'

Somehow it lowered down the roaring and started to observe us. I continued getting frightened at its enormity. I had to overcome my fear and started remembering Mrs. Morgan's words of making eye contact with the animal to scare it and then sudden bulleting in the air made the gigantic animal fall unconscious. A crisp tap on the left window with a sharp voice asked, 'Are you okay?' I couldn't spell anything out.

Morgan said, 'The animal should be placed in my car, for that need you guys to help.'

I strictly said will not get down while the two went out. I asked them to shut the doors properly. They then gently positioned it in his vehicle, he added, 'this is a rare breed of Jaguar you won't find in our home.'

Once everything got set Sania took the driving seat. I swiped my position with her inside without stepping out of the car.

Our destination point was Chris' home, we reached far late to them. Raj said 'Hey Sania your right knuckles are injured. Why did you take

this trouble? You girls should trust Sonu's driving if she drove we boys would have become second.'

I then literally went to him to thrash, 'You didn't know what was happening with us. Why didn't you wait or look for us?'

He politely replied, 'Babes, We were in a race.'

I sat to relax at one spot in the garage. He pumped into me, 'Why are you so tensed?' I told him about the dreadful incident.

He reacted, 'Would have given the engine for its appetite.' I replied, 'How does it eat that?'

He replied, 'You guys should have first induced it inside the car, then jump out leaving the object to its prey.'

I said, 'How can that be possible. You are a weird dynamic person.'

'With Teehee.' with a smiling face he reacted, 'It was a joke, see you are slowly forgetting about it.'

Isha alerted us saying, 'Uff I wonder how Rose will react to this.

I don't want to be caught, taking off this stuff is to unfocus the damaged areas. Shit man, her most favourite belonging is badly wrecked. How to fill up this glass? God, you are my dear saviour.'

Chris cackled, 'You are making things hard on yourself for clearing it as though you are trying to get rid off some murder evidence' and then he scrutinized the top, sideways and inside and remarked, 'Even God cannot rescue you'

She checked, 'Why?'

He showed and spoke with high importance, 'Some of the pencil designs has been crushed that were dropping from your satchel.'

She then worriedly replied, 'Oh! The important one Sania has to present is spoiled. This reference actually was needed to be developed on the clothes.'

He asked, 'How long will it take for you to redo the sketching?'

She said, 'Not a big deal, I can sketch from the scratch.' And then she started to do it. We explored inch to inch for the missing drawing portions to ease her job. All of us involved ourselves in her work. Suddenly, realized the entire garage has turned into a workshop. The chief material for the attire is made from bluebonnet flower.

When the epitome was ready Sania said, 'This can be manageable. I would like to skip wearing earlier designs for this dress, it's not at all difficult to wear and can flip off from those complicated fringe long gowns.'

Isha replied, 'I know that baby. That's the reason I have come out with this new design.'

Late evening Rose had come and was shocked to see the garage's new shape. Our day turned out to be good. She was planning to take the car out and from her observance, she spoke, 'These craters are from Jaguar's paws, let's cut the glass to this setting. We were so happy and surprised at her declaration and even she cracked jokes and made funny looks like the animal Jaguar tempted at seeing the Jaguar Land Rover.

Raj added, 'This woman is speaking like me.'

She appreciated Isha's handiwork, 'What a lovely design? By the way who is the presenter?'

Sania replied, 'It's me. I would be promoting this design though not so confident how it will turn out to be but I am gonna do it.'

The event turned out to have great exposure on my friend and a sense of challenge for Sania but ultimately it gave huge fame to both of them. They were tensed though Isha covers up to be not. For her more than this project, faking her feelings for Chris while in love with him was far too bothering.

During the trials, our pretty Konkani lady couldn't balance herself on the blue shined eight inched sharp pointed heels. Her hair messed up like a bird's nest while she walked fast to cover-up the matter consciously with the high stand cut out open toe. Raj immediately said to knock off the heels and wear the blunt sandal to the same platform. Isha with a high pitched voice said, 'Don't break. That doesn't go with the outfit so let it be as it is even though she is not comfortable.'

The magnanimous opening ceremony took us to another sphere of glamorous existence. The whole setup by itself is a style extravaganza. A set of six sleek Italian models exhibited Isha's feather fringe stone embedded long gowns. Each one of them was fashion themed iconic beauty pageants and were lineage from essential fashion practice so has that distinctive line of stylish presentation. They were symmetric, pleasant and had bold appearances. But Sania in the front seemed like the fashion stigma was madly imbibed in her and this place is just made for her. Her outlasting looks took away the pulse of the viewers. The style modulation and the subtle expressions shown by her made you feel she is different from Sania. The inconvenience happened to her at the backstage didn't see during her walk. The tender nervousness turned out to be a super smartness on her face. She stole the show completely. Through her high sensibility, the bluebonnet attire was prominently shown. Looking at her I imagined her like a beautiful princess rambling in the palace. The Cavos event announced the best five presenter couture that would go for the next level. It was not so shocking to hear Isha's design take the first place. 'It's Goddess worship for a nascent fashionista like Isha under Stella. You find her as a best guide, critic and driving force.'

At the announcement, Stella was extremely happy and shown the pride like a teacher who feels for his student's achievements. Offstage, she exclusively praised Isha's work. She said, 'Sania's exhibition is authentic while gracing your art fused with refreshing creation. It's a perfect maven fabrication. So intensely touched by your shrewd blending style that showed classic designer's common sense.'

I was shocked when I saw Sania taking her two amputated sharp hard stone sandals beneath her that was hidden in the dressing chamber and dropping them in the trash. I was about to say something to Isha then Raj tightly closed my mouth with his big hands. I understood that he might have done to secure Sania's confidence during her ramp walk. I wanted to tell him that I will not say anything to Isha but he didn't give me a chance. He held me hard and took me to a corner, he started to laugh seeing my eyeball moves. While releasing he said 'You have such big eyes man.'

I said, 'I know. How did you do that?'

He narrated like a movie sequence, 'We checked Isha and found she was with Stella. During that course asked Sania to engage you in her hair-do. That time I and Chris grabbed each one pair did specialist spoil. When we informed our model she gave us a one million dollar's worth smile.

'You are so childish Raj, what if your activity would have turned into failure.'

Raj replied, 'Ummm childish aaaaa! childish aaaaaaaaa! Let me show you and suddenly came very near to me. And whispered in my ears childish aaaa! I could feel his erratic breath. My heart was pumping fast as I have never seen him so close involving only a small margin of our thick clothing. I replied with mixed feeling breathing heavily, 'Umm' and I wanted to come out of him.

So I said, 'Isha you know what?'

He slid away then I said, 'She is not here.' But actually, there stood Sania.

She asked, 'What's happening guys?'

He replied, 'Shouldn't check out the obvious things.'

I smiled and said, 'He is scared that I would reveal to Isha that you walked with the plain sole.'

'Hey, please don't do that.' And mentioned gladly that I have time for the next challenge. Till then I can breathe.

Surprisingly Chris and Isha were also there and I was not sure if they heard. Seeing my face Isha felt something was wrong with me so before she opened her mouth Raj said, 'She is thinking of that animal.'

I looked at him and expressed with my face that should I reveal the truth, showing some facial gestures. Chris reacted, 'Still scared?'

Sania expressed wrong feelings and said, 'Gentlemen you both don't know but we are still feeling the shivers. You have no idea as to how that magnificent creature scared us. We cannot explain to you.'

Isha winking back said, 'I feel Sonu's fear is a different one from the three of us.'

Raj looked at me and asked, 'Is it so baby?'

I reacted, 'I don't have any fears, instead I am having a heavy feeling for some untold incident.'

He immediately said, 'I know what you are trying to say but this is not the time to reveal that. We must be in high spirits upon winning the show and even Sania accorded with him.'

Isha said, 'I will be waiting to hear from anyone of you. Hope nothing is serious?'

He smiled and said, 'No, Absolutely not.'

It was almost late night and I was waiting at the cascade for Raj as he texted me to come. It was snowy and foggy with mild drizzling. I was just having my sweatshirt on and suddenly there were hands, which were covering me with a pullover that was giving me warmth and relief. I turned around knowing it's him but then I skipped my heartbeat for a moment looking at the beautiful white bouquet of Claire Austin. With a smile, I took my mobile and showed his picture. I said, 'Do you remember this person who got a bunch of roses for me despite the rain.'

He smiled while handing the bouquet over to me and said, 'Let me tell you this is my next phase of love.'

There was an utter silence, which was only filled by our eyes gazing at each other and all we could hear was the song from the mansion. Soon he asked, 'Do you like to have a moon dance now.'

I replied, 'I feel you know my answer already.'

With the flow of music, we started to dance. A feeling of happiness rushed throughout me from his first touch of romance. It was happening like a dream to me. After our moon ball, he walked with me to my room.

Once we reached, I gave him a goodnight gesture and he placed his head on the corner of the door and asked, 'Do you really want me to leave?' I gave a big smile and told him goodnight and closed the door.

He whispered through the door, 'I know you are still there.' I responded, 'The ball dance is over, now you can go.'

That moment Raj broke the silence by saying, 'All I could hear now is just my heartbeat and it says I love you.'

Then he said, 'Sonu, I love you a lot.'

That time I held the doorknob even more tightly with happiness and I couldn't control my big smile, still having my eyes closed.

He said, 'I am leaving this place. Goodnight my princess.' I was there until I could hear his footsteps fading.

It's one's destiny when you bond to a stranger who has a true love for you. Raj's visit was not expected but his presence led to an expectancy. Time has come for us to depart. I want to be with him and spend some more time with each other. Somewhere, I felt I would miss this guy after my return to India. He asked me what were my plans as soon as I land in Mumbai? I told him 'Well, the very first thing I would do is to sit with my parents and tell them that you would be my life partner. So when are you guys planning to get us married?'

But I didn't actually express my feelings to him and instead, I said, 'I would look for a job.'

He asked, 'What sort of work would you prefer?'

I said, 'Something that excites me and should have something in common with my passion and talent.'

He gave me a romantic gesture and with longing, he asked, 'Baby, Can I hug you?'

I reacted, 'Really?'

He repeated, 'Can I hug you? A mild touch?'

I looked into him and said, 'Just a warm comfortable hold.'

He did a capsule hug stating I need this till I meet you next time. And spoke too emotionally, 'I am leaving my princess with a heavy heart. You please take care of her. She is a very normal girl as you are. She is as sweet as you are. She is as true as you are. And you know she is my love.'

There were really short of words to express my feelings for him. I just showed my happiness through my watery eyes. He soon tightly hugged me melting my tears and said 'You should also know one more thing, she is as sensitive as you are'

I said, 'Hmmm you are right and she will miss you more than you miss her.'

Then holding me harder he said, 'Smile babes. You have something from me and gave enclosed in a greeting card. He asked me to open it after I reach. He mentioned, 'I like to convey my feeling for my loved ones through letters. Since childhood, I exchanged so many of them with my friends and family. You should be reading this.'

I reacted, 'You are different from our generation.'

He smiled, 'I actually got this habit from mom. She usually communicates with us through her writing. You know I have all those saved to my collection.' Then Isha stepped in with a mood of missing us and hugged him, saying, 'Hey Raj this is a friendly one, different from Sonu's hug. Well, some damage to yours is fine would appreciate that.'

He reacted to her with a smile and then looked at me. She said, 'Sonu didn't say anything. You made me realize not always to think too professionally. If you were not there I would have failed to understand Sania's confidence is more important than anything else.'

He said, 'Thanks buddy and you should grace Chris as well since he was also equally responsible to break her heels.' And where is he by the way?'

Isha replied, 'Today is Chris's dad's death anniversary so he went to offer his prayers, I would be joining him shortly. Since you guys are leaving I have come here.'

The sad moment had come when the announcement was heard from terminal 7 that the flight to New York was all set to take off. I saw his face with the expression of losing him. He was also equally feeling like me. He held my hand and said, 'Baby don't worry we shall meet soon. I feel very bad to see you like this. Please show me your happy face.'

Still, I cried without stopping. Isha couldn't control me as well. He cracked jokes saying, 'Glad your teardrops are so tiny if not letter note would have become salty wet smudging my words for you.' And then gently did one last hug saying, 'Pretty girls don't cry. They make their partners bother for them. So darling let me do my job to weep for you. The craving thirst for having you in my life.'

I smiled, 'I will not stop you, Mr. Raj Verma, kindly go ahead with your mission.' And that's all I have seen of him for the last time.

******

The most notorious, ridiculous and crazy person had come to pick me at the Mumbai Airport. I smiled but he didn't smile back and instead threw my luggage at the back seat of the car stating, 'I was left with no option but to become a driver for you.' Then he tried hard and failed to take the letter, which I was holding. I spoke, 'You know bro, my return journey was absolutely boring.'

He didn't react. I again repeated then he said, 'I heard it, please don't resonate the same thing.' He slowly attempted again and this time he was able to take it from my hands.

I did uff! and said, 'Hey idiot don't dare to open, it has Raj's personal message to me.'

He laughed like a devil saying, 'See you are gone now. It's already in your smart brother's charge.'

I pleaded with him, he literally treated me like a slave to do things for him after we reached home. I was instructed to get into his room to clean his stuff and I did it. Later, had washed his bike which was kept like some old dead man's vehicle left in the garage for ages. After doing my best he was still unsatisfied and asked me to wash the tribal dress that he had worn to surprise his friends. He went in disguise in that tribal dress to scare them, so now asked me to wash that. I was terribly tired due to my travel and now with this unexpected awful service. But that's fine as I can do anything for those beautiful darling words by my love.

I told him, 'I have done even that and now you don't have anything to assign so just give me that letter. He did smile like a monster and said, 'It is out of my hands, don't actually remember where it was misplaced.'

I got super angry and was about to break his favourite antique black horse. He screamed 'Don't do that will tell you. I kept it at the place where we usually put letter cards and envelope posts.' Before he could complete it I went running to check. There were hundreds of variety of letter notes, invitations and all. I searched and read the first two, interestingly one was a card from Raj's parents and the second one was from Sam's dad Raman uncle. I then went to mom, showing the cards.

She replied 'My favourite boy Sam is here. So, be ready to attend the welcome party along with us.'

I reacted saying 'I will come but what is this invitation card from Raj's parents?'

She replied, 'It's an invitation to their village on the day of inception to cultivate food crops by doing farming .'

'Oh is it? Wow mom, when is this?'

She looked at me and said, 'Don't be so excited beta, the date would be mentioned afterward. In that, you can see and moreover, have to tell you that we are not going there .'

I asked with a dull face, 'Why, mom?'

Dad had come up hearing our conversation and intervened, 'You guys better stop talking about them and their things, as those are not entertained anymore .'

I was shocked, 'I am not understanding what you are saying, I was about to express that I cannot imagine marrying any other guy except Raj .'

His face has become red while speaking, 'He should also have that sense to marry you. Such a rubbish person. What did he think of my daughter, just a dating material?'

I told, 'Dad, I am really not getting this.'

He then showed his mobile incoming call records and said, 'Raj's parents called to convey that their son is not ready to marry you. I said to them then forget about my daughter as well and don't dare to trouble her. Neither you nor your stupid son.'

I replied, 'Dad I feel Raj is not that kind of person & I am being confident on this as per the moments we had in London .'

Dad left me saying, 'I cannot tell you anything beyond this. It's up to you now.'

Mom continued, 'Raj just wanted to date you and was not committed for marriage. His parents said he is not reacting or responding when they spoke about it. Though they are a modern family this characteristic of him is not expected .'

I didn't consider my parent's words to be true because I still feel Raj's love for me is a serious one and therefore did not want to impose any negative opinion upon him. His nature was something I fell in love with. So, I wanted to listen from him what mom and dad had expressed. I telephoned him but he didn't answer my call. In periodic intervals, I tried connecting with him but couldn't reach him. So left a message stating, 'I heard from dad that you are not ready to marry me .'

The party had started and by the time we arrived. Dad's and Raman uncle's common circle was already present. Mom strictly said, 'Don't look upset and try to look normal as if nothing has happened to you.'

I said, 'Will try mom.' At first sight, Sam seemed professional with the greyish slim fit blazer while uncle announced, 'I am glad my son is back to India. So happy that he would be in his homeland.'

The arrangement was as such every guest was offered an exclusive table. I sat as per the family's nameplate that was displayed. My mood was not at all proper. I just wanna scream loud. Sam noticed me from the dais and came to me with a beaming smile, 'Hey Sonu sweets, how are you?'

I shook his hands and said, 'Welcome back Sam .'

He replied, 'Ohhh!!! You heard that let me tell you something but it's confidential, I am travelling back without saying to anyone.'

I reacted, 'What?'

He replied, 'Yes, you heard it right. I have come here for a while.' And he gave a decent look at me and said, 'You still look super cute as you were as a kid. I still have that glimpse of you in red and white skirt uniform and your typical captaincy as a head in charge of class sports. Hope you remember our 4th and 5th school days.'

I replied, 'Of course, by the way, you are very brainy and my parents used to take your name as a reference and say study like him.'

He half smiled and showed guiltiness while he spoke, 'Actually I am a drop out from Stanford.' And hesitatingly continued, 'I formed a rock band out of my interest in rock music. To start this, I discontinued my education .'

I reacted, 'That's awesome. I admire you more for this. You should consider yourself to be lucky for being able to try out your passion. It's very rare to get a chance to pursue one's dreams .'

He then gave shocking expression and said, 'You are the only person from the circle of my friends and family who appreciated and shown positivity. You know this silly celebration dad intentionally organized is to make me get fixed here. Before anybody could ask anything he says my son is back so hearing that I will not go to New York again. And I don't follow any of them. As I go with the feelings of my heart. Everything in life should be 'khud ki marji.'

When he mentioned New York I thought of Raj's city. A sudden message from him, 'Baby was on the island, didn't get time to check your messages and calls and had a signal de-link.' I was tensed so asked him to reply for what I had texted, he replied with an immediate 'Yes.' Then teardrops continuously started falling on the mobile screen taking off my vision from it. Sam got concerned and handing over a tissue, asked, 'What happened?'

I didn't respond to him, I seriously wanted to break my phone while Raj was calling back to back. I came home in the middle of the party and following me even my family had to leave. I fell flat on the bed sobbing badly and threw my mobile. It showed Raj's last text message, 'Did you go through my letter.' That time Dad visited my room and spoke angrily I didn't like your behaviour at the party for coming off so suddenly. Check this, here is the proof why Raj didn't commit to marrying you, he is in a relationship with another girl.' And he gave the letter to me. I saw his face and tore it and flowed the pieces into the trash.

Dad then said, 'Your 22 years of experience of life wouldn't be enough to make you understand about a guy more than us. You deserve a better person than him. Just forget everything that happened to you.'

I couldn't take the situation as simply as how dad told and was walking on the lawn in the midnight. My bro saw me and asked, 'What are you doing here at this odd hour? Come inside.'

I replied, 'Will sleep in some time you go.'

Then he said let me walk with you. His face showed some serious concern. Never in my life have seen him that way.

He spoke, 'You are thinking of Raj right? I know his memories are bothering you. I understand you have become very emotionally attached to him. I strongly feel he is not a flirty or dating kind of a person who denied to marry you. There must be something unsaid. Why don't you meet his parents and understand? And I regret couldn't read the letter before dad had taken over.'

Raj's village has a green moth widely spread across the place. This land is mostly greenish because of the impure water stagnated in the ponds. Snakes are crawling everywhere without any fear of humans. The villagers ignore these reptiles when they pass by. They react normally as if it is nothing unusual to them. They were so patient and cool to direct me to his home. I had to repeat multiple times the address to make them understand my pronunciation.

A middle-aged lady who was draped in orange coloured golden border saree and had jasmine flowers tied hair bun first noticed me. She is his gorgeous mom. No wonder why her son is so handsome. I would say he has got the charm from his pretty mom. She recognized me and was giving continuous smile watching me and checked about my parents if they had come. I replied, 'No I have come here by not informing them. They don't want me to have any more relationship with your family. The same would reflect with me as well but want to confirm something before I go with their views.'

She held me gently and took me aside to a private place and in short spoke about her life. She seemed emotional to talk about it. Thirty years ago I got married when I had no idea what it was all about. I was very shy and not an outspoken girl. For my husband, I seemed like an ignorant female as I didn't talk much and also could not utter a single word in English. The only reason why he married me was for my beauty. As preferred by most of the Indian boy's, pretty girls are mostly sold for their looks. I happened to be one of those. Few months after my wedding we had to move to the US for his job purpose. Suddenly everything turned out to be new for me right with my husband. I started to learn things to keep up the pace with him. One day he expressed, 'Why don't you work as both of us can fulfill the growing needs.'

I got him but to take up any job there, I should be knowing the foreign language. Though I didn't know the English language I still didn't feel disheartened. If I am not a strong woman who doesn't prefer to feel bad for herself than to take up the situation as a challenge. I would have been a big failure. I learned the language with great difficulty and was able to get work as a spokesperson, which was not so easy for an Indian who is not native of United States of America and could maintain my dignity with pride. 2 years later Raj was born and soon after that, my two daughters were born. Somehow I didn't like bringing them up in a foreign land. So powered my guts and fought with my husband that our kids should study in India no matter whatever it is. And I always told my children the importance of our culture, traditions and relationship values mostly to Raj because once married he would be a head to his family leading all of them. So do you think I will miss out on this important aspect and grow my son to be a person who doesn't know the importance of bonding? If you can notice his nature it is very straight forward just like me and his approach to things are emotional and even this is like me. He prioritizes more to other's feelings and you know what he said?, I can marry no one else other than Sonu. She would be my lifelong partner. But something is taking him off for giving the commitment right now. We have told to your parents to give us some time to settle the things and understand him, but they are rude and least cared to listen to us.'

When she finished saying, I asked her openly, 'Is your son dating some other girl?'

She immediately said, 'He actually started to live independently from us and it's with his female friend .'

I reacted, 'Living with a girl, how? I and my family should take this?'

She undoubtedly replied, 'They both are close friends. Just in case if they are in any relationship Raj would be gutsy to marry that girl. And he wouldn't truly say Sonu is my marital partner. And I am very confident my son is not such a disloyal person to date one girl and marry some other.'

And after giving some pause she continued, 'See I understand my son as a mother and I am putting across the matter to you to give it a thought before you decide anything else.'

And she surpassed, 'My husband's ancestry did farming. I always have a dream coming here to extend this profession. But he was never fine with the notion of us quitting our respective jobs. I explained to him many times that we can stay with the family and facilitate the village to turn green. He was reluctant and so stubborn that was back of building a sophisticated empire with the money earned. He became a greedy man but fortunately, that didn't come to my children. They respect and value people's feelings than any other materialistic possession. Actually, before coming here, we were in Canada in a green spot. Now I would say that was for a good reason. My husband was amazed by the plant growth and aesthetics. He told me will shift to India completely and continue with the family legacy of farming. When I expressed this to Raj he was shocked with his dad's decision.'

Her husband came with booklets and gave brochures to her stating,

'Usha just a few are remaining, keep it safe.'

Those are their business stuff of the business that they do in Bangalore. He had seen me and asked, 'Are you Sonu?'

I replied, 'Yes.' Then he showed some excitement while responding, 'Need to talk to you, just come along with me.'

We were walking in a paddy field. I was wondering, 'Why this couple was addressing me separately. Let's see what he gonna talk about?'

He showed me his neighbour's flourishing crops and said, 'Indian farmers have best practices but they majorly lack monetary support and water supplements. If we can seek to them providing in adequacy those things that they need then India would be leading in the front.'

I replied with a smile, 'Yeah.'

He asked me, 'I got to know you are good at people management then why don't you take up that position in our recent establishment and oblige yourself in our business development process.'

I looked at him with an awful face, 'Does this person feels his son met me to validate my abilities to support their business.'

Then seeing my expression, he continued, 'Raj said not to force you for any if in case this role is not fine for you we would be setting a new industry as per your convenience.'

'An industry' of my liking.' I didn't know how to react to this. So far nobody asked me, 'Hey what's your interest, will start a venture accordingly.'

I again smiled, 'Not like that. In fact, I'm quite happy that my interest has been offered to take up but have to consult with my family before I go finally.'

He saw my face with a strange look, 'Your job should be of your choice that defines your career so if you are fine they have to be fine.' I thought to myself how my parents will react to this open offer?

At the breakfast table, dad asked me the previous day where did I go as there is dark blackish green smooth mass stacked to car tyres.

Bro sighed to me not to say anything but I didn't feel like lying to dad even though I am sure he would get angry. Still straight away said to him, 'Went to Raj's village.'

Dad had dipped an idly piece in sambar but paused to take into his mouth while he spoke, 'After so much explanation what made you attend that function?'

I replied, 'I didn't go for that dad. The celebration had almost got over by the time I reached.'

I feel concerned for you as a father so indicated you strictly as to why we have to maintain our distance with them. And by the way what for you visited?'

I then smartly mentioned about the job offer put forwarded by Raj's dad. My bro looked at me with a face showing the expression, 'Why didn't you say this to me, idiot sis?'

Dad laughed, 'That family is insane. I don't want to even comment about them. What are they actually expecting from you ghar khi bahu ya kuch aur?'

I said, 'Dad on a serious note, tell me should I join their business?'

He reacted, 'You have to decide on that. I don't want to poke my nose in this. First, they wanted you to be their ghar khi bahu now kaam. Patha nahi unko kya chahiye?'

I believed this is the right one for me so showed my gut spirits and travelled to my favourite city, Bangalore.

I entered the office space with a notion to make the couple understand that their son is exploratory towards relationships and more than anything this was in my head. I took up this work for the same reason. My cabin looks were depicting absolute bliss. The walls had pink and white shades, which is my favourite combination. Admiring at it, I sat on the chair and soon the VoIP instrument made beep sound that showed a call from Raj's dad, 'Sonu, relax for some time. I will make you meet with the teams shortly.'

I replied 'Okay uncle', but then I corrected and said, 'Fine Gyandhev.' followed by 'ji.'

He said, 'You can call me Gyandhev.' I said, 'Ummm, sure.'

All were looking at me strangely when I was introduced. They felt I am a young girl who gonna take some big responsibility.Two interesting personalities who remained back came forward and shook hands and introduced them as Vaidhya and Megha. One casually said, 'I love being funny and the other said I spread happiness around. And we have one more in our team who is busy at the desk.' And mentioned with winking eyes, 'She is also like us.'

I asked, 'Pardon!' Then they made a strange laughing sound and said, 'Actually we are so spontaneous for brass tacks .'

I acknowledged, 'That's cool.' and looked at them if they can say something.

'Shhhh! The agenda of hard work is to do sheer work', whispered Vaidhya.

'You know "The Art of Living" is for the sensuous mind and body. If you can balance both then no matter how much the stress, you can handle that stress with ease when at work.' remarked Megha.

A known voice called out, 'Guys kindly stop making us feel bored with your nitty-gritty' and dragged her chair towards us. I was shocked to see Ikya here. I had closely seen her face one more time. She spoke, 'Hey, what a surprise dear. Are you the new joiner? Sorry during your welcome I was on phone conversation with our MD's son.'

She continued, 'Guys we both need no introduction. We know each other already.'

Vaidhya said, 'Uffff never interacted with him. You never introduced?'

Ikya corrected, 'Oh God I am talking about me and Sonu. You want to speak with him, let me call him right now.'

He didn't pick at the first ring so she re-dialled switching on the speaker button. He answered in a hurry, 'Ikya, I am heading to the hospital on emergency, anything urgent drop a message.' She replied, 'Okay Raj.' and kept the call.

Immediately they got concerned. A female creaking was heard. 'It's midnight over there what would be the reason?'

Ikya reacted, 'It sounded like a labor pain might be taking a lady to a health center.'

I behaved as though I was not interested in the conversation but actually there was an inquest running in my head as to who could be that girl? Sometime later I felt to fairly acknowledge the situation of a person being in hard condition.

I checked for credentials to access the computer. Uncle ji has come. He informed, 'Ikya, let her get familiar with this place.' And seeing my face, he asked, 'Are you comfortable?'

I said, 'Yes' and swallowed the word 'Uncle.' It was difficult for me to address him by name.

Driving back to my apartment, I messaged Diya would be late because of heavy rainfall. The parking lot was flooded with water due to which heavy blockage happened. There were chaos and continuous bashing all around. When I looked at the surrounding vehicles, they were too close kissing one another. Luckily nothing happened to my car. It nearly took an hour to come out.

Mighty girls waiting at the exit gate literally jumped onto the seat and screamed, 'Finally we are out of the premises.'

Soon I was asked, 'How was your first-day experience.' Ikya said, 'Guys stop bothering my friend.'

She asked me 'Acha tell me something how did you join here.'

I didn't answer. But I asked the same question to her. She replied 'Raj was the reason, he insisted me to quit the earlier work. He mentioned, friends should support each other. And I liked it.'

I said, 'Looks like he is a bonder to friends.'

She spoke, 'He is a champ. I just admire for what he is.' I didn't know what to say.

Vaidhya said, 'Let's do something tonight. I don't want to go home. Let's become crazy feminine.'

Megha said, 'Hey what did you just say. Have you heard my inner voice? I was about to say let's, party girls.

Ikya explained, 'I don't recommend that as we have to work tomorrow. Let's wait until Friday. The weekend is the perfect time to relax.' Megha reacted, 'That's fine, we shall manage. let's make it Ikya.'

She nodded with great difficulty, I took right turn considering her gesture as okay and finally while heading towards the street of pubs she said 'Let's go back.

I didn't reverse the car and asked, 'Why so?'

You remember the last time we partied I waited for my friend for hours. He is Raj by the way. I couldn't meet him that day. Like now even that day it rained. So rain and the party is a bad combo. Will plan it for some other day. Vaidhya reacted, 'Oh lady of this generation having fun is like a bicycle if you don't peddle it you end there unmoved forever.'

I didn't get the complete essence of what she conveyed so accorded with Ikya and was back at home. My dog leaped on me and walked half legged seeing me. I expressed, 'My loving morph, you miss me so much.'

Diya spoke, 'You realized that when your pet had to show up half legged. Now, what else should happen to make you understand your loved ones are missing you a lot .'

She was angry on me as I didn't talk to her or update her about anything post my London visit. I wanna cool her down I said see the weather outside. There was no response I asked her, 'Did you trouble yourself to prepare something for me?'

Her diction was, 'yeszzzzz, I cooked.' And harshly took my mobile to order something for food home service.

She immediately gave back saying, 'You don't require phone just dump it. No problem if you don't answer mine. Oh God, check this always you have some hundreds of unattended calls.'

I saw the screen, there was some unknown number that I missed out to take several times, as I kept my phone in silent mode.

Next day at the office.

I was in the elevator when received a call again from the same unknown number. It got disconnected by the time I picked. I almost bumped into Megha while looking into the gadget as I didn't have any sense who was coming from the front. She stopped me and said, 'Hey lady, be conscious. Then she again asked, 'By any chance were you also there at the pub boozing yesterday.'

I said, 'No, so you guys went.'

She reacted saying, 'Of course we did that. Now you don't declare to Ikya because we gonna again go on Friday. Let's not miss that.'

I acknowledged with a smile. She then asked feeling intrigued, 'With whom you are busy on phone 'Boyfriend?'

I said not really and got connected to that number.

A familiar male voice said 'Hello.'

I asked, 'Who is this, I received so many calls from you.' He laughed and said, 'My name is Sam, your friend.'

He asked, 'Are you fine? The other day you were upset and down for some reason.'

I said, 'Yeah! but I am fine now.' He again checked, 'Is everything alright with you.'

'Ya, Sam. I am absolutely okay.'

He reacted, 'Cool, I have something to say. I am going to perform Indo- western fusion in the coming Friday night. My band has come from abroad. Since 2 weeks we did musical sessions on Goa beaches. We played some street music with modern composition, this facilitated to another chance that you can watch it on day after day. And you have been cordially invited.'

I replied, 'Congratulations! Sam. I am so excited to make my presence there but I am not in Mumbai.'

He said, 'Guess what? This is happening in your city, will share the venue.'

I smiled, 'Okay my dear friend.' And while finishing it he added, 'If you are interested to see the rehearsals then you can come by that day morning itself.'

Was passing by the steps when I closed the call. Megha blared out someone at the stairs.

'See, she climbs 11 floors man. She doesn't want to use the elevator to put down the kilos. Is this the right way to reduce weight?'

I saw Vaidhya. She seemed like she gonna faint off taking heavy breathe when she said, 'Miss. Concern, do you think I find it good to burn calories like this? I was trying to catch the lift till the 10th floor but then realized have one more floor to cover for our office and finally, I got rid of my hangover.' And mentioned Ikya would be late to the office she texted to drive the call by ourselves.

I had no clue about that, this is my second day at the office. I was just observing them how they gonna do. They two jointly spoke about the business and dealt with the customers for product promotions. It was made as a short discussion while Megha kept the ongoing call on mute and whispered, 'Let's dial to Raj through Ikya's machine .'

Vaidhya held her tightly and said, 'Let's finish this and do that.'

When they were done, the hands went onto IP telephony and got connected to Raj. They seemed damn crazy. Megha rolled the wire-like noodles and was holding the phone upside and said that she was not able to hear anything.

She spoke to herself, 'Oh lady, why you are in a hurry and not put it properly.' And while doing so said 'Hello' with a sweet voice.

Vaidhya immediately whispered, 'Get the modulation like Ikya.' Megha did it and left the phone with the speaker open.

Raj responded, 'Ikya just hold on' and spoke to someone, 'You wetted my clothes.'

Vaidhya continued to whisper, 'He is talking to his pet I guess.' And checked my face.

I said, 'No idea.'

A heavy breaking sound of glass and liquid splashing was heard in the background. Raj's voice was relatively high, 'Cera! You again did it. Now see what I am gonna do. Let me roll these ice cubes on you.'

Cera! (an investigative weird expression was shown by two)

Megha said, 'God they are in private time let's not disturb them and disconnected the call abruptly.'

I was taken aback and tears started clouding my eyes. He was intimate with a girl and I couldn't bear him sharing his personal space with her. I didn't want to analyze their relationship. My possessiveness made me hate him and also her for no reason. I cried very hard hiding in the restroom. Why have I become so mad to him? I didn't like the way I am going through so consoled myself and checked into my cabin.

Ikya was there inside and she immediately said, 'I just came.'

She checked if I had jotted the summary of the client call. I said no dear but I can tell you what all was discussed. She felt so happy and asked, 'Would you like to be part of our team?'

I reacted with a smile and said, 'I am okay.'

She replied, 'But Mr. Gyandhev said you are good at human interactions so thought you will prefer that.'

I said, 'This is something, which is of my interest as well.' She reacted, 'Perfect! And left to inform him.'

I didn't know why but my body severely ached and I was having a high temperature. My eyes were swollen and became red. I came off suddenly in the afternoon took the prescribed medicine and slept off.

On the blossoming refreshing day, I recovered from Thursday's sickness. Ikya's message was the first text I read, 'Hi Sonu, Good Morning. Please engage the call as I would be late to office.'

I saw Diya's face and thanked her for taking care of me like a baby. She reacted, 'Friends are there for each other so don't show formalities and upset me. Bye, I am leaving. Don't forget to take tablets. You should be under medication till you are completely fine.'

Her response threw me to Ikya–Raj bond.

I managed to be at the office on time. Both the mighty girls were already there. They were quiet that day. Looked very dull, which is not normal for them. I asked, 'What happened? Why you guys are silent?'

To make them active I said girls we can speak to Raj, Ikya would reach office like yesterday.

Megha said, 'Not today! Usha Gyandhev is there in the office. She is an .Ironclad lady. Fun Friday will turn into funeral Friday.'

I laughed and said, 'then can expect the call to be more productive.'

She reacted, 'What do you mean? We just do fun at work not fun with work.'

I laughed again and said, 'Wow! You know I would be joining your team.'

They exclaimed in chorus, 'Awesome! No worries please do the due diligence of Ikya's absence and our presence.'

I said will do it from my cabin and was about to go when Usha Ji instructed admin person to inform me to come to the discussion room. I walked in and she dazzled me with her beauty. First time in my life, I felt, I should be like her in my late 40's age. She used the discussion table as a display of eatables and said, 'This is all for you. Have prepared it exclusively for you. If you are okay you can share with others.'

I could feel mom's homely feeling with her. She forced a few items to have then. I said will have the remaining post the call.

She asked, 'Which one?'

I replied, 'Every day 11' 0 clock schedule status call with the client that is driven by Ikya's team.'

She immediately took the phone receiver and spoke, 'Good Morning! Past two days Ikya is late to the office any reason?'

I could see another woman in her, a professional who is ensuring discipline to be maintained.

She kept the call and told me if you are taking the lead of Ikya, just attend here itself and can have this stuff simultaneously.

I controlled to show my laughter said, 'Okay good to go.' I opened the bridge linked to client telecom line spoke about the services that we provide in terms of technology than our competitors. I could be better in convincing them as few of the instances, I didn't know how to project that we are better. Once it was over she said, 'You didn't sound like you are new to this system. Well executed.'

I reverted with a smile and collected the stuff and stepped out of the room. Almost all eyes were on me. At that moment, they might have thought I am opening some condiment store.

Megha signalled, 'Hey Sonu come here, did Usha give you this?' I said, 'Yes.' And offered them.

Vaidhya with sweets in mouth, 'You joined a couple of days back. How did she give to you man? You know that woman not a single day of her life smiled at any of us.'

I reacted, 'She asked me to share with you guys.'

Megha said, 'Might be in Ikya's absence she would have given to you.'

Then I realized girls are meant to be for gossiping no matter whatever is the topic. I openly kept the foodstuff on the side of a table. One of the other colleagues asked, 'Did you meet Arjun?' For the entire last week, he was on leave.

I said, 'No I didn't?'

I was pulled to his chamber. It looked like I entered into a world of calculus. All possible number stuff you'll find right from simple addition to algebraic formulae. You can see the discrete circle and square imprints. The gaps in between are filled with numerical designs and there is an 'alpha' shaped weighted mould that occupied the middle section of the tablespace. He was not there so waited to get introduced. I was astonished to see the room abstracted with signs of numbers.

Mighty girl, Megha said, 'All these would reveal he is very much fond of mathematics and to add, he even calls his son as, 'Beta. It is algebra, Beetaa.'

We were leisured for him looking at the demented creation. She spoke with tiresome, 'I guess he left early to let me check'. And simultaneously spoke, 'Where is Ikya? Are we going, today? What about Friday party?'

'Oh shit! Tonight I have to attend a musical concert?' 'Hey! don't rush, who's?'

I said my buddy, 'Sam.' 'Just wait.'

I asked, 'Why?'

She mentioned, 'Would like to accompany you to the concert.'

We three started just after that. The happening was at the palace grounds, which is on the other side of the city and since couldn't escape from the traffic I spoke in a dispirited voice, 'Sorry Sam my bad will be late.'

Megha said, 'I never heard of this name. Is he a famous personality?'

I reacted, 'No he is still anonymous who dropped out from Stanford.'

They spoke at once he should be crazy to give up education at such a novel institute for music. A rockstar can only do this. I had to avoid signals to reach fast. My phone rang, didn't bother to pick as I felt even that can slow my speed. Finally arrived and in a hurried voice two of them said, 'Let's get in and show the entry passes.'

I was clueless, didn't know where we are heading. Somehow entered into people passing by public got exhausted. An inducing sound jazz beats, drum rhythms, acoustic guitars fused with the raving chorus was heard. I was having goosebumps listening to the song synching with the instruments played. We were present in front of the viewing screen noticeable from the musical platform. I observed the music band alternating on the sound devices.

Vaidhya asked, 'Is that Sam with black stubble beard?' I nodded with, 'Umm.'

She reacted, 'He has a sexy voice.'

Megha got overwhelmed, 'He is so hot man.'

Sam dispersed his eyesight all around and announced my name in the song, 'Hey Sonuu Heyy Sonuuuuu! Come here, buddy! Come sing along with me.'

Vaidhya opened her mouth when he did this. Then I was pointed by him, the crowd cleared the way and allowed me to reach him. I was tensed, didn't move. Megha gave a gentle push to go there. He came half the way pulled me onto the dais and gave the wireless mike to sing along with him. Sensing my nervousness, he engaged my voice with a catchy tune that boosted my confidence and was able to sing with ease. Slowly I picked up the hard version of it unknowingly I could finish up the song. After that, I went down with a feeling of accomplishment. I felt some magic happened now.

Vaidhya said 'You sang well, didn't expect that you could do.'

Megha gave my mobile and said your phone rang, just check. I saw Ikya's missed calls and a text in our common group named crazy girls, 'Guys where are you I am at the cocktail lounge.'

I showed them and they said, 'Shit man!' And checked their mobiles too.

Megha politely asked, 'She is there. Right? Shall we go.'

I replied, 'You guys please carry on and gave my car keys.' And then I waited for the concert to finish. I was lost, totally became music maniac. How much to express the talent they were showing up. Along with Sam, six other guys equally mesmerized. I mostly get his glimpse as a geeky guy who is dedicated to studies, not into other activities. Once he was done with the show came running to me. I don't know he was sweating like hell. 'Should I give tissue to wipe?' I asked.

He said, 'That's fine' and questioned back, 'How much you scale me for this.'

I replied, 'You are beyond anything Sam. I can say there is no scaling meter to rate your musical artistry.'

His expression was so cute, with a smile he said, 'I am overjoyed my best buddy liked it. Are you not active on phone ringed you many times? By the way, you look so pretty in this Salwar Kameez from there you were shining especially with these two twinkles. And he came close by, 'Let me feel them.' And touched my Jhumkas. 'You know I was able to identify you in the audience because of this shimmer.'

I reacted with a blushing face, 'Thanks.' His co-musicians came calling Sam from afar and took the guitar which was on his back and said, 'Dude let's pack up and leave.'

Sam then introduced me to him, 'She is my childhood friend.' That guy smiled and mentioned, 'I know her name. She must be Sonu. We heard that on the stage man.'

I also smiled and said, 'That's correct.' He then left saying come soon dude.

Sam then asked, 'What's next? What's the plan? Did someone come along?'

I said, 'I have come with my two colleagues, they went.'

He interrupted, 'So you are waiting for me, my goodness. Now I will not make you stretch more. Let's go.'

He took me to his changing room back of the stage and was surprised to see it empty, he then phoned to his friend, 'Dude I see nothing here.'

His friend responded, 'We cleared your stuff also and left the premises. So you happily come with your friend, enjoy the ride man.'

Sam reacted, 'But I don't know how to drive on these traffic roads.'

I controlled my laughter and replied when he kept the call, 'Hey I don't think so there will be much conveyance now if you have issues don't worry I can do the driving.'

His reaction was cool then we walked to the carport. He wore seat belt firmly and said, 'Drive safely, can't understand these people. They simply avoid signals.'

I smiled and said, 'To reach the concert on time I did the same.'

He was clogged, 'Oh shit you don't do that now. But then he saw my face and said, 'I trust your driving, let's move.'

This made me remember Raj's expression when we came back from Morgan's place.

'You guys should trust her driving skills.'

Sam checked, 'Why delay? Please start.' I then put the gear to accelerate the vehicle. Keeping aside London memories I spoke, 'So how is Raman uncle?'

He replied, 'Dad is fine and will be super fine as I completely dropped my plans to fly.'

I reacted, 'How come?'

He took pause and spoke with smiles, 'When I have support from my dearest ones like you why should I go back to New York.' I showed my face that sounded like oh really? Is it so?

And mentioned, 'Life is too short man. Do whatever you like to do.

In the end, you shouldn't regret.' He smiled, 'Well said, my disciple'.

I did eyebrow raise, 'You are not Swami Vivekananda to follow you, just Sam.'

He replied, 'Yes an ordinary guy who is trying to prove that he is something!'

I said, 'You will Sam I was just kidding. We are at the heart of the city now tell me where should I drop you and go?'

He reacted with concern, 'At this time dropping me and going to your place alone is not safe buddy. You check into my place tonight.'

'No, Sam instead we both can go to my apartment.'

He said, 'You live with your friends, don't want to disturb their privacy.'

I didn't respond so he mentioned, 'Let's have dinner then you can decide on next'.

I said, 'Ok.'

He then enjoined directions to a Villa where he was residing that was located in the lakeside resort. It had a beautiful view the waterfront looked dark brown in the night. The big semi, 'o' extension on the top floor attached to his room had a green garden where puppy rabbits were in meatloaf positions. When I went to them they ran fast and I couldn't catch them. I sat there with a pout face. He smiled, 'Come in buddy they are not in the mood, will bother them in some time.'

I asked, 'How long you will be here?'

He asked, 'Why? and while going inside he said, 'Not sure depends on the upcoming concerts schedule.'

I replied, 'This place is so pleasurable I want to play with those cuties.'

And was about to unlock one door. He instructed his friends would be there in the connecting rooms so don't open. Immediately I took off my hands from the latch. He then held my shoulder made me sit on the couch and said watch my recorded shows and switched on his laptop. His tracks are in English mostly melody. I started to sing that spoiled the original song. Suddenly heard some metal dropping sound. I went through the dining area to him. He was quickly keeping washed meat aside and collected cutleries from the floor in a bowl. I saw him and checked, 'What's happening Sam?'

He replied, 'Should we dine buddy? I hurried to make some vegetarian dish since you are hungry.'

I reacted with a face of surprise, 'You cooked!'

He continued, 'Actually due to this reason, I don't prefer hotels to stay as I want the kitchen to cook by myself. You don't have to worry I deliver five-star standard foods.'

I then said, 'I am okay to try non-veg today.' He was shocked, 'Are you sure?'

I continue to hum one of his songs that I was listening to. I sang loud it has come out like goat's voice.

He laughed, 'You gonna take that boiled animal flesh. Are you sure you will have?'

I replied, 'No I am scared.'

He pulled my legs, 'I eat meat which is dead. You eat alive ones so you are experiencing these weird voices.'

I asked innocently, 'What should I do to get rid of this.'

Here is the solution dear and has put earphones in my ear. He mentioned practice to these Spanish songs of mine.

I said, 'Will put high volume to understand the meaning of the song. He reacted, 'Strange buddy! If it is loud you will understand the lyrics. I never know this.'

I felt silly went to the living room from him. I randomly looked around my eyes caught one of the corners where colourful magazines were zig- zagged in the bookshelf.

I asked him, 'Can I go through these?'

He has come to simplify my search, 'You can read this London publication.'

I said, 'Hey Sam didn't expect this from you most of them are fashion digests.'

He asked with an exclamation, 'What do you mean!'. I meant mostly women's particulars.

He reacted, 'Oh Gosh don't make me feel insecure. You know one of the temptations that provoked me in recent times is this.' And showed one UK journal.

There was a British model on the cover page spotted in ethnic Lehenga who was portrayed like an Indian bride. Her beautiful wrinkled hair almost reached her knee. Her fascinating appearance matched with some familiar person's whom I know. So I soon flipped pages to check the inside story to the biggest surprise. It was about Sania and her designer Isha.

'Oh my God! Oh my God.' I screamed, 'My girls are famous now.' And reacted at the pictures. This time Sania's major challenge would have been with long hair.

He asked, 'Do you know her? She is one of the trending models in England.'

When I said, 'Yeah.'

His expression showed like he was on top of the World.

Seeing his excitement, I made a phone call to Isha. I asked her to convey my hearty wishes to Sania for marking on London's fashion and modelling.

She replied, 'How did you know this?'

I sarcastically said, 'You shared it right the achievement of you both?'. She reacted, 'When! It's been a long time we did speak.'

I replied, 'My friend, you should realize that you missed out to share this important update?'

She reacted, 'This happened a week ago and I am surprised how did you get to know?'

Sam being anxious sighed, 'Are you talking to Sania?'

I smiled at him while I replied to Isha, 'It's a turn-up to find through one of the magazine reads'.

She mentioned, 'Oh, is it? I didn't know this is in news so soon.' And then enquired, 'How's your sweetheart?'

I sounded unheard to respond'. She repeated, 'How's your love?'.

I bluntly didn't answer her again. She then asked directly, 'How's Raj?'.

With annoyance, I reacted, 'I don't know?'. But within a split second, I had chilled as seen Sam holding two baby Rabbits coming in front.

'Here you go.' placed one on my shoulder. 'And for more fun let me put this on your head.' He was sitting it that delicate instance stuck me to feelings of Raj so I shouted, 'Will you stop this Sam. And pushed him with my right hand.' He politely went away taking the two away.

Isha's voice questioned, 'How come you don't know? What's happening there? Who is Sam?'

'I shouldn't be so aggressive?'

'Why Sonu? You better calm down.'

I then replied to Isha with poised voice, 'Dear, He is our classmate. I feel you both don't know each other since you moved to Delhi for your primary education. At the same time, he had gone abroad to pursue his. He is a very talented budding singer. Sometime back his concert was finished. I am with him through that.'

She said, 'That's fine dear. Have fun. We can catch up some other day.'

And kept the call.

I was too harsh. I went to apologize. I am sorry Sam I was bull spirited while I behaved so. His humble gesture qualified him more. With a smile, he took his guitar, 'This is for you. A song that heals your pain, a song that brings a smile on your face. Lyrics flowed. You are a happy soul and gifted to be one.'

His friends joined from other rooms. They sang a Spanish song that has a meaning of, 'Oh beautiful lady, always wear a smile. It is like a rainbow to the sky.'

I blushed and blushed when Sam sang in English for me. He was so happy about seeing me. I then asked, 'Now I want cuties.' He winked if your mood is fine they have to be fine.

After that awesome night, I woke up very late the next day. It was so lovely I was surrounded by grass where baby rabbits were around. I was about to take them from Sam's hand standing at the bed spoke with concern, 'Have breakfast. Then only anything. You should be punished for skipping yesterday's dinner.'

I denied it to pamper them. He came close to me, 'I will feed. You can play.'

With the crumb in mouth, I complained about the ingredients he has put. I want only simple stuff. He removed all of them and fed with plain food. Once done he asked, 'You want some more?'

I said, 'It's yummy. But I have eaten to my capacity.'

Whenever I check my mobile there will be hundreds of messages and calls. Let me go through Diya's text first,

'You have to be responsible. Where are you?'.

I replied, 'I am at Sam's place will be coming in some time'.

And the next message was from Ikya, 'Last night it was too awkward. These two addict drinkers gave me so much trouble.'

I then spoke to Sam I need to go, buddy. He then mentioned, 'Cool I will drop you.'

I replied, 'I guess in a plane because of no traffic in the air.' He said, 'After your driving experience, I gained confidence.'

I gave directions to Ikya's place. I was confused because I hardly visited her home. With great difficulty to trace we reached. I said to him drive back safely and leave a text if you are alive.

He replied, 'You are so mean. You should be alert on mobile to get acknowledged.'

I took the staircase to the first floor and then rang the bell. Ikya's mom opened the door. I greeted her.

She replied, 'Please come in. My daughter went out with her dad. In case if you come she asked me to give your car keys'.

I took and went back home. That morning while travelling to the office I was listening to Sam's recordings when I spoke to mom. She heard dad having a conversation with someone about my marriage. I told to mom, 'Ask dad not to condition and be obsessed with it. I need some time to come out of my love.'

I greeted, 'Good Morning Ikya! She looked distressed. I asked 'what happened'

'That Friday was a nightmare. They were fully drunk. To pull them into the car I had to plead them. You know they puked on the road. I was scared of what if cops come. I didn't dare to drop at their places took them to my home.'

And she continued, 'It's good since nothing happened. I heard from them you didn't come to the concert. How did it go?'

I replied, 'Yeah it was expected. My friend Sam did an amazing job with his singing'.

I showed her the video that I captured. She didn't complete to watch the full performance and continue to speak, 'You know our mighty girls common crush is committed in love.'

I asked, ' you are referring to whom?' She replied, 'I am talking about Raj.'

That moment Vaidhya came & heard what Ikya said and spoke looking into me, 'Hope you don't mind if I date your friend Sam. He is so charming.'

The conversation continued between them. She checked, 'Who is that girl Raj is in relationship with.'

Ikya reacted 'An angel from heavens.'

His soulmate is in fairy tales, Oh God he lives in a fantasy world. Ask him to come to reality. The problem with rich kids is they have too many unrealistic fascinations.

Ikya clarified 'She is there in this real-world just that he treats her like that.'

******

A sudden phone call woke me up from my dream.

'Will arrange my travel as soon as possible and kept the call.'

I stood from the bed for quick action, due to the dim blaze of light, did hand slip on alarm clocking doll placed on the table next to my cot and it broke into pieces giving huge sound then Diya in her sleep turned her posture from left to right.

That time, I came out of my complete sleepy mode but not from the shocking news. I enabled internet button and managed to book morning flight. Without understanding what I was doing, booked cab.

Reached airport, was rushing with the boarding pass, did big hurry with no clue. At the check-in, one smart lady was pleading security officer these hot homemade laddoos are very important. I prepared for my son who is away from home. It's been six months since he is put in the hostel. My bad have forgotten and carried in my handbag. Please don't put in the bin. He was reluctant to take her request and mentioned ma'am you are not supposed to carry edible stuff in hand luggage. Losing hope, she was about to move from there while I comforted her and spoke strongly to him, 'why are you so obsessed with rules. Can't you allow something of no harm? Do you think this is the only mode of transport? Save back her stuff, will seek other routes to travel'.

He commented, 'How can she take that when it is already put in the bin'.

Lady boldly put her hand inside, took out her sealed laddoos and replied to him, 'You don't understand this.' And left stating, 'That's fine. I will go via train'.

Don't know what went through his mind. He called her back and said, 'You can travel this time, these will be allowed'.

She was happy, came to me and said, 'Thanks for the stand and voicing my opinion. Though I lost hopes you stood as a support.' I replied her, 'If you want things to happen, try till the end'.

And had to leave her as my flight was on the verge to take off. Luckily able to board last minute. Instructions were given to switch off mobile before I did have seen unread text message 'Come to church's front gate'. and that reminded my visit to Mumbai.

Saint Andrews church stood majestic and marvellous as it ever could be. I entered Church through an arch of white roses that brought out the wedding mood. I could see a few business partners from Chris close circle and some of our close friends arrived there. In spite of acknowledging their presence, I was only concerned about Isha. Soon she saw me hugged and wept terribly. She was flowing down with emotions.

I reacted, 'Don't cry. You should be happy. You and Chris are becoming life partners. This is the day you both have been waiting for.'

Despite the decors and fun mood created by friends, she couldn't frame a sentence and responded in tears, 'I am getting married without my parents consent.'

Dadi made her presence there and showed verbal gestures to cool down our bride.

I wiped her face and said, 'Isha you should be delighted. Neither your parents nor you are possible without your dadi. With her presence, here consider the blessings of your entire family are upon you and there is nothing for you to be guilty".

Hearing my words, she spoke with the delighted tone, 'Yeah I know. My dadi is awesome.'

Grandma asked me to accompany her and spoke, 'Thanks for gracing your friend's wedding. A bride's close friend presence is as important as the groom. Her parents were too stubborn to understand their daughter's feelings, but I cannot ignore my granddaughter's happiness.'

I was speechless to see dadi's commitment and love towards Isha. She continued, 'I am old, not sure how long I would live but as long as I do I want Isha to be a happy soul. And this would only happen if she is with Chris. So with the support from your beloved Mr. Raj, we decided to get them married as a private affair. And we have plenty of time to face the later consequences.'

With a shock, I turned to Isha's face and she nodded, 'Yes, Raj encouraged dadi to make it a secret wedding and on your behalf, he did a lot more to us being a mere acquaintance.'

I was off and my inner voice questioned loudly, 'When? How did he ever understood the seriousness of marriage and stood for my friend's love.'

My eyes rolled for him, 'Where is Raj?' And I did find him in the front rows starring at the ceremony hall. Being unsure if he had noticed me, I went and stood very close as I don't want to be ignored. I was immediate, just two centimeters distance to him. Checked again if he had noticed yet and he still did not. I was wondering if he was doing it intentionally or he was busy doing nothing.

My phone buzzed and it was my parent's call. I was wondering if I should pick it up or not. At that instance without even turning to my side he said, 'Don't pick' and then he continued noticing my face, 'If you can lie that you are not in Mumbai attending Isha's wedding just go ahead.'

'I don't think that there is any need to hide this from my parents as they would understand.' I replied.

He reacted with confidence, 'No, they don't. They are too conventional to understand this.' With a loving smile, he locked my hand with his fist. And said, 'Whatever you reveal, ensure Isha is not into troubles. At least let the wedding finish, then you can answer.'

His hold became gentle. I was about to take my hands he then did strengthen and made it a firm hold. And was looking at me with a cute expression. I had to put force to get rid of him and with a serious tone, I said, 'Raj, you don't know my parent completely. Maybe their beliefs are old but far better than your philosophy towards a relationship. Don't worry, Isha is my best buddy and I have my responsibility to safeguard my girl's situation.'

I looked at my phone, put in silent and dropped it inside my hand bag. I then turned out, 'I must fulfill my very important duty as brides' mate.' And walked towards Isha, giving him no time to respond. He stood there with no clue what just happened. Dadi delighted over the wedding came close to Raj. I guess grooms' mate should be too". Wasting no time, he gave a big smile to dadi and stepped close to Chris.

Raj winked to Chris saying, 'I guess everything is going on smooth.' Ankur jumped in between from nowhere a camera posing as the photographer, exclaimed, 'Yeah, seems everything went well.'

As the church father made his presence everyone took their seats with me and Raj standing right beside the couple and Ankur busy in taking pics. The father recited the holy rituals and made both Chris and Isha take their vows. And they exchanged their rings followed by a gentle kiss to seal their marriage. Raj came close to me and thanked me for withholding my parent's call and said, 'I know you will take care of your friends very well.' And with hesitation, he enquired, 'Where is your buddy Sam?' My inner voice questioned, 'Why is he checking about Sam? how did he come to know?'

He added "I thought you might take him along" and his words annoyed me. I replied with pride" unlike others, he is busy in fulfilling his commitments".

Everyone greeted the couples and after all the selfie's and groupie's the couple wanted to have a special photo session with us. Raj stood behind and did a pose holding my shoulder. I said 'Raj' he tried to be casual when he redid the same with a firm tone I said, 'Raj, please off your hands on me.' He walked away at my response.

Isha reacted, 'Why are you being so rude to him? If I am married today it is also because of him.'

'Isha, I know he is the reason but please stop being on his side. There is something understood about him. He is a person who likes to date denies to marry. Honestly saying he is sweet as a boyfriend but shows shit to marriage.'

She ringed, 'Hey Raj, where are you? I am sorry for letting you go.'

He answered, 'You need not make an apology.' I came off being upset with my love.

She replied, 'I understand how it feels when loved ones misunderstand us. Its high time to confess her what you feel. Hold things before you lose.'

He said, 'I did share my feelings through letter and it never come back to me.'

Isha said, 'Raj, I could talk to her, make her understand your love but accepting or not is on her hands.'

Isha mentioned to me after their conversation, 'I could feel his love for you. He will stand for it.'

That is the problem he is so misleading. I don't have any strong point that he would get married to me. She stopped me and said, 'You have to be patient in a relationship. Might be marriage is not a quick call for him. I have faith in him and a truly deserving guy for you.' And she mentioned that she is flying back to London on the same night and dadi would try convincing my parents.

On my flight back to Bangalore, Isha's words were resonating in me and I kept thinking, 'Should I not condition my love to Raj? Or should I?.'

The question was simple but the decision wasn't. After a long, exciting, emotional and tiresome journey, I reached home and landed on my bed. I closed my eyes, and everything felt like a dream. With a smile, I made my decision to give Raj my unconditional love. When I looked at the time, it was 12.05 AM and my day got special not because I was born but because my love for him is reborn. With a lot of messages and calls flooding in, I responded with excitement and happiness but neither Raj nor Sam called or texted me and it made me wonder if they had forgotten my birthday but eventually slept off. As soon as I stepped into office was overawed to see roses binged on the floor, in the lift, bay area, on the escalators even in the office compound. Looking at me my dear colleagues did gracious smile a singular person has arranged on your birthday babe. I bleached with happiness while entering my cabin. Now here it is full of rose bunches. There was no small inch space to place my feet. I got teary-eyed when I saw the wall with my family pictures. And there was a card placed on the table with a note. I was excited at that moment did a big noise, 'I am waiting, waiting, waiting, waiting and waiting to read.' I did with speedy action as I don't want to miss out like the last one. In full swing, I started to read that feeling of my guy the emotions I was undergoing are my delicacies in love.

Hey, Birthday gal.

You are very special to me not just as a friend but also as a true character. Your genuine nature made me fall for you. And my beloved these beautiful roses expresses my love for you.

Your's Sam.

My hands picked up the phone ring when I said hello. The immediate response was I thought you wouldn't receive my call. Then I realized, 'It is Raj's tone.' Without any delay, I reacted 'Yup, Tell me'.

He wavered to express, 'Today is very close to my heart.' I went crazy that he would wish me. Though the reason is obvious to me I asked him back 'Why so Raj?'

You know I met Cera on this day while I was young. As a chubby kid, the cutie expressions she showed are so adorable. I still remember the first glimpse of her and can never forget the darling looks of her. And the journey continued so far. Our togetherness is celebrated.'

I stopped him there to cut the call. Whenever I make up my mind there comes a painful hatred for him. The one whom I wanted in my life is just going back and the one I see an as good friend has expressed his love to me. I can see through the cabin glass door, Ikya's gestures saying something to mighty girls. I little opened it. I heard her, 'Really this whole thing is done by him I thought someone else.'

Megha expressed, 'Last night he was here to complete this setup. We have been notified by Arjun to allow this.'

Vaidhya whispered, 'Shhh! Let us go and get the birthday girl. They rushed towards my cabin.'

Soon my eyes were closed with a thick red satin ribbon. Then I was left free in the room where echoes are heard. A masculine voice slowly raised.

'We grew along passing each other's shadow around.

Never realized when my fighting bug turned to the angel of my grandma's story. Every new thing comes to be old but my love for you is feeling that makes me bold. Life with you is a 3 AM dream, I would never miss. Being your moon partner would bless me with peace beyond the sky.

'Hey, let me see you.' He came to my back his fingers went through my loose hair. He turned me to his front while removing the knot. And soon blasted the balloon that has twinkles. They have flown on me like a shining river. He then knelt with a rose 'Oh my princess. Will you marry me?'

The three suddenly pumped in and said, 'Your confession is open now.

We are also here. They overdid for seeing me.'

He was in that position for some time I don't want him to be embarrassed so nodded with a smile. Mighty girls celebrated that moment as their love is accomplished.

Megha reacted, 'Hey Sam if you are not committed to Sonu I would have dated you.'

Ikya was very unhappy throughout. She even didn't involve like other two. Her mood was off for some reason I couldn't attempt to check.

I reacted, 'You guys made my day.' And Sam I continued to say.

He mentioned, 'I am not done yet, sweetheart. Have something else for you.'

I pestered him with one question, 'Where are we going, Sam?'

He commented 'Oh my talking parrot. You will know we are just a few miles away.

We halted at his villa's garage he said to get down the car. I looked into him and asked 'Why?'

He reacted, 'My doll you have too many questions.'

He closed my eyes with his gigantic hand. I said, 'No Sam. Again, what's this one more?'

He made me walk till upstairs. I could hear some whispers going on

'Wo aa gaye. Jaldi karo.'

That was my dad's voice to my mom. I was about to slip my leg. Sam supported and said, 'Buddy, almost done.'

Mom wished me with a birthday song. Raman uncle also joined their singing. Once after that, I said to Sam, 'Such a sweet surprise. I didn't expect their presence.'

He mentioned, 'I know what makes you happy.' And he disappeared the cake hiding behind with his hands. Suddenly the cut one occupied my face like a facial and the grandeur black dupatta, he did shade with colored cream. I angrily ran behind him to apply back. When we went to the garden he said with heavy breathing out he held my hands.

'We have one more rabbit added now. Let us get naughty.'

I took my revenge by rub in my face cream made his black denim jacket cheesy fabric. He removed it saying I still have clothes inside babes. Uncle watching us has come, 'Enough Sam, don't ruin her clothe.' And gave a saree to change. I wore it and while

I appeared wearing it Sam said, 'You are making my mom's presence being felt.'

Uncle announced with a threshold, 'Hum bado ne milke tum dono ki shadi fix kara hai.'

Then Dad asked my shawl I gave. He placed on Sam's shoulder and said treat this attire as Sherwani. With tremendous happiness, he has put in front rings to exchange. I was in shock saw my mom's face she opened her speech with smiles 'We would be happy parents with your marriage.'

Sam gestured to give my ring finger, looking at me, he gently held my hand from down and rolled ring on my finger. My eyes were wet when I had to put for him.

Mom expressed her love for him, 'Beta, your character keeps our families pride high.' And mentioned, 'You both are made for each other.'

Raman uncle took the pitch from there, 'Sonu is awesome. Because of her my son has got some stability.

He is settling in India just for her. So lucky to get a daughter in law like her.'

Suddenly, there was a mobile ring on my phone. It was next to Sam. Seeing my nod, he picked the call and spoke. I was tensed at his expressions. Once the call was over, I asked him, 'Who was that?'

He said, 'A call from car showroom that your vehicle has been left with them. And the person is waiting at your apartment for the deliv-ery.'

Dad asked me, 'Did you give it for service? How do you use? Are you still careless rider? Do you bash while driving?'

'Wait, dad, my car should be in my office basement. There is no chance of this unless someone takes it.'

Answering him, I was about to ring Diya if she was in flat. Sam stopped me and said, 'Let's go and check. Don't call her.'

I reacted, 'Chalo.' And while we were about to leave uncle said, 'You both are in a hurry. I don't want either of you to drive.'

Dad mentioned, 'Raman Ji, I will take Sonu to her place.'

His driving was at moderate speed. He felt that I don't follow signals.

So, explained about the rules. How he does usually.

At the apartment, two girls were anxiously waiting for me. Ikya's smile conveyed something to Dad. He reacted, 'I will wait in your flat.' And mentioned Diya to take him to upstairs.

I questioned Ikya, 'What is happening?' She replied, 'Come with me.'

I asked her, 'Tell me. where is my car?' She said, 'It is in the next lane.'

I asked her, 'Why there?'

A brand new car covered with red roses was there. She asked me to get in.

'Hold on Ikya. Why should I? whose car is this? Again, what is happening?'

There was a guy with white shirt and blue jeans inside. He stretched himself from driving posture to open the car door. When he did it, he said, 'Oh my God. You look damn hot. Happy birthday, babes. This is for you. Please be seated we shall go.'

He came out and said to Ikya, 'Thanks for bringing her.'

And gave some loving looks to me, 'Let's move. I need to talk to you.'

Ikya was following him.

I told her, 'You don't know the things between us.'

She immediately said, 'I know everything and that everything has everything.'

'Come babes let's have a loving day.' And pulled my hand. He felt the ring, 'Oh! this was not there before'.

I was pissed off, this man shows damn interest like a partner. Giving close look I spoke, 'I and Sam are engaged today.' And with pride, I sat by myself, 'Chalo Raj, will see what you wanna talk.' With a fierce face, he started to ride. There was silence from him he didn't speak for some time so I broke it by asking why are you not with Cera for your celebration? He didn't react and the silence continued. Then with a sarcastic flavour, I said, 'Hope you guys did the most to make this day more special.'

He replied, 'Yes, we have some striking moments. She has travelled to

India with me. Mom and dad are taking good care of her.'

'I hope, they will make that poor girl understand about you.'

He thrashed the steering with force, 'I may be a mean to you not to her.'

I said, 'I wanted to go out of you. Could you please stop the car?' He denied doing until we went to my apartment. When we reached he stopped the car and asked me, 'You can leave now.' When I got down he shut the door with huge banging. That moment portico lights were turned on. Even Diya and dad had rushed down to check if something happened on the street.

I couldn't move then I realized my saree was stuck. I tore some portion to walk away. He controlled himself and asked if there is any hurt on my body. I could see from his eyes that he had resisted his feelings.

Dad came in front of him and spoke, 'You again have come to my daughter's life. Before I become abusive, kindly move from here. And remember this, don't grab the attention of her when you fail to afford her.'

Raj had nothing to say back. He left us showing his impulsive action by driving the car with double speed.

Immediately, Dad reacted, 'His impression and name would be erased henceforth.'

And asked me to pack all the clothes to travel to Mumbai. I stuffed my baggage with a heavy heart. While leaving, Dad invited her for my wedding with dates to be confirmed.

She excitingly hugged me to congratulate. Curiously asked, 'Who?'

When I spelled Sam's name, she said, 'There wouldn't be anything happier than your best buddy turning to a life partner.'

I smiled to acknowledge her statement. We were travelling back to Sam's place. I was dull and upset while dad said, 'Stop going to the office hereafter. If you ask me the reason. I would say, him.' He then looked into my eyes, 'If you still thinking of him, you are fooling yourself. You should know this. Raj doesn't want the pleasure of being coupled like a husband and wife. This man falls in love being in it sincerely disagrees to make her girl as his partner. It makes sense while a man marries his girl to carry their love to a bond where they can make them companions. I feel Sam is this.'

I said, 'Dad, I feel love is the augmented form of like/interest. It just can't happen at first occurrence unlike it happened to me with Raj. Now, whoever is in my life. It needs some quality time to quantify him. If this works, our love pertains.

He reacted, 'You take time to move on but don't bother yourself thinking about Raj. I am telling you, Sam is a nice guy. You have to be loyal and love him unconditionally. As I say he is a gem of guys.'

I do remember, Dad was saying similar words about Raj and his family before I met him for the first time. It was late evening. At the space in the living room, there was a setup for a live DJ.

'How's Ikya's car present?' Sam overwhelmed.

I was silent. Dad answered, 'It was a surprise that overturned to a shock to her. By the way, how did you come to know?'

'Uncle, I was the person who answered her mobile and informed in another way.'

The happiest person of the day is mom. She came with mithai's to me and said, 'I have stored in the box you can take to your flat and have.'

Dad said, 'She will come with us tomorrow.' And corrected his sentence. 'If in case, Sam is also coming both of us can come together.'

Sam replied, 'No uncle, I am planning to travel to Africa for my next concert from here.'

He then concerned, 'Sweetheart why you look this way? The day is not finished yet. Let's party. He offered red wine. The boys started to sing along every sip. The song sounded like a sad breakup version. Dad was constantly observing me so I ignored his looks. He came and reminded about my tomorrow's travel. Surprisingly Sam said, 'I would like to take you to my concert with some pause what do you say, uncle?'

Dad reacted, 'I am okay and she should be on toes to come.'

Sam looked at me, 'If you'll come, I will not miss my love. So stay back.' I did nod, 'Okay.'

The immediate morning did goodbye to mom, dad and Raman uncle. After that, I went to flat Diya was brushing her teeth. She saw my face as though an alien has come. I told her that have cancelled the visit to home as I would be travelling to Africa with Sam.

With half done with mint on her mouth, 'Oh girl. How long?' I said, 'Maybe a week or more.'

'How about work?'

I replied, 'Dad said to discontinue the job as I may redo the memories.'

She concerned, 'I can understand but you don't mind me for this. Yesterday in midnight, Ikya came checking for you. I didn't say where were you. She didn't ask for details. Just handed the key of new car.'

I said, 'You didn't do anything wrong but if I was there I would have not taken.'

******

July 25th.

'Baby come down. I am at your basement.'

I hurried to set the things when I sided my luggage. I felt I am carrying overload. It's his concert and I was with more stuff. But then I patted that's fine and went down.

He giggled, 'Good that I have asked my boys to leave. You know this is just slightly more for one.' He quoted sarcastically.

Watchman complained about Diya that she parked the car in other's space. Sam started to laugh.

I said, 'Don't laugh let me get the keys.' He was still laughing like a kid.

I said, 'What's there to laugh so much.' I was looking around where did she put.

He was consistently laughing & said, 'Have seen it outside.'

This time I couldn't control. I went out of apartment portico. He asked, 'How are we going to Airport? Through cab, is it? Let's go in this.'

I asked, 'Are you sure?'.

He imitated me, 'Chalo.' And dumped our luggage.

The way he did, I laughed like hell. He reacted, 'This is the first time, I have seen your full-on laughter. I am more than happy, you know.'

I opened the car door thinking of something. At my leg space, there was a piece of silk. I had to pick up since he also noticed. He immediately said, 'Oh God! That's the reason why the Saree looked eaten. I wanted to check where did you break.'

I said, 'Sorry Sam, I know how much this means to you.'

He replied, 'You mean a lot to me more than anything else. Don't worry. I have saved many of mom's sarees. Those all would be yours. And said please continue.'

I asked, 'What?'

He replied, 'Your smile. The sounding laughter you do.'

I did rainbow shaped mouth while dropping a message to Diya, 'There is a complaint from apartment management that you are troubling them by occupying their space for parking. I am punishing you by taking off this car to Airport. Please get from there.'

I showed to him what I texted. He said, 'Why only till the airport, we goanna fly off in this.'

I asked, 'What's wrong with you?' After some time there was a mobile ring from my roommate. I picked. She said, 'Oh Gosh! I am lucky, you lifted at the first ring. Where are you guys?'

We are almost at the end would reach shortly. She kept the call. I was shocked. Like a traffic police, she stopped our vehicle at the airport highway. When he put the break she opened the door and pumped in. I reacted, 'Why my day is running with two weirdos?'

Sam said, 'Leisure buddies have so much time to check-in.'

Her looks were too suspicious. She asked him to park in one place. He did the same. We collected the luggage. He dragged his things simultaneously and called his boys. They were late than us though started early. That time she took something enclosed from the car. She said, 'Uff! You know, I was so tensed. Glad that Sam didn't notice though.

It was there to be seen. It is how it was kept.' I asked her, 'What is this?'

She anxiously revealed putting it in my hand luggage, 'Raj left in the car for you. Now it's up to you if you want to read.'

And whispered, 'But you know?' I asked, 'What?'

She said in emotion, 'I have read this. Then Sam came back to us piled my luggage along with his.

I said, 'I can manage mine.'

He reacted with a smile, 'You come with ease babes.'

She hugged, 'You don't know. I was super worried, came here at high speed. My purpose is done. I will leave now and screamed, 'Happy journey guys.'

High up above the sky travelling through clouds, I was lost into thinking.

Sam suddenly asked, 'Why can't you pair with me as we don't have a female singer.'

I replied, 'Please Raj, let's not spoil the show.'

He was like, 'Did you rename me? I heard something.' 'Yeah! I said you are king of music.'

Then he smiled, 'You are my queen.'

He said holding my hand, 'King and queen make sense.'

We sheltered at a tribal place. Kids around were excited to see some new faces. Out of shy, one of them hid himself in my skirt. I struggled to make him come out of it while they felt strange when Jose was taking their photographs. I said, 'This place is quite remote. It's difficult to stay.'

He explained the motto to choose that.

'The people here are living in below poverty line. Most of the children are malnutrition since they don't have basic needs. So the money we earn will be spent on these for their livelihood.'

I appreciated, 'You guys are awesome. Actually, Sam wants me to sing for the girl's voice. I am apprehensive. I don't think so mine will sync?'

He reacted, 'You are so sweet. Just imagine we six boys performing

midst a girl on the musical podium. It's a heavenly scene man. You will mesmerize the crowd.'

I smiled and said, 'Should learn the singing to make it lively.' He smirked, 'You have to do nothing. Just be present between us.'

We walked to the practice session that was happening in a grime hut. He said to other guys our female vocalist will be Sonu. They were like cool and gave lyrics to learn. They were playing the instruments to get the fusion that distracted me?

I said, 'You guys rock. I think I have no complaints.'

Sam was laughing as he understood, I can't judge. He came to me, 'Your part is to behave like a doll with some lip moment on the stage.'

I was offended. So replied, 'Can do better work and Jose already told

this.'

Sam saw his friend. That guy reacted, 'I spoke what I felt dude.' Then

there was a smile exchange between them.

'Sweetheart, do look into my eyes.' He has taken the violin to his arms curving me with his body he said you sing, I will strike these strings for you. I was too closely circled by him. His arms were touching my waist while playing. I learned a few lines. Now, I have forgotten those. He spoke in my ears, 'Sing babes.'

I was nervous. I did stammer to say, 'Don't remember the lyrics.' He said, 'Then sing with me along with the violin tune.'

He was going on because of that I became conscious. My lips were tightly shrunk. I slowly open up & I spoke, 'Can't sing if you lock me this way.'

Immediately with a gentle gesture, he came out of me.

I said, 'Do I really have to learn like this?' He smiled, 'What do you expect from me?'

I reacted, 'It's a big statement, Sam. I just want some positive energy for the show.'

He replied, 'You will gain that if there are several sessions like this

between you and me before the concert happens.'

I said, 'In that case, I choose to stand like a statue uttering some lyrics.'

His friends amused while he controlled to show it up.

He spoke, 'There is a treehouse nearby that does magic. It was laid by two African couple on their symbol of love. If you climb on that, you will get power. It's the most visited one.'

Then I showed some interest and said, 'Can we go now?' 'The souls remain there. So you may induce their energy's.'

Before he continued further, I had forced to move. To the most disappointment, the person who drove our gypsy, in which we had come was missing. The vehicle turned out to be horrible as the roof was gone.

'Dude, it will be hard to drive. Don't think so anyone of us can pull on this deep soil. We should go with a driver, who is an expert.' 'I can do that.' My response shocked them.

'Are you not feeling that you are driving the bullock cart?'

I clearly said, 'No.'

'Hmmm. Looks like you are very much excited to meet the souls.'

I replied, 'Of course.' And asked him, 'Have you been there before?' He replied, 'Yes, I even spoke to that couple. They are so a dry warmth.' 'Aww! You are so lucky.'

He said, 'You are my reflection.'

Once we both were there, I realized what he said was complete shit. There was a tree with branches reaching the soil.

I was too serious when Sam said, 'Let's crawl.' You caught my ignorance. So happy right.

He looked into my eyes, 'My love, this doesn't have any importance. We shall make it.'

Just after that. At the roots, we were dropped insanely into the watery soil bed. I could manage to float my head in the air while rest was immersed in a loosed dirt pit. My bottom flair floated on him. His teeth were brown when he said, 'This is so hilarious.'

I didn't open my mouth. With close shut, I spoke, 'Let's try reaching the top.'

'You are crazy queen. Let's move from here first.'

We swam a bit till the dry land. When I stepped out I was shivering. He immediately shielded me for the warmth. Once I was fine he freed me and checked for my handbag. I said it was sunk along with us. He went back to get.

He probed into the girl's treasure. He found tissue bun. Immediately he cleared my cheeks and said, 'Baby, I can't miss seeing your pretty face.'

I blushed and went to wash. He gave his hand, 'let's climb.'

Waving branches made me feel cradled in his arms.The silence of our love was jolting pearly gates.Dream of being a bird was gratified on the roost of the tree fort.Pitter-patter melody of romance made me boogie down like a queen bee. Liquid sunshine over the leaves was reflecting he is all mine.

******

Practice day 3

'You look kickass. Had so much fun yesterday. Were you shaken with her?' Jose asked.

Sam: 'Dude it's always fun when you are with your girl. I was silly but enjoyed being that.'

'I have practiced. I can sing lines. Play the background.' I said. They did with applause.

'Babes you are smart without my sessions able to make.' That continued with their laughter.

Rock show

I looked like a mermaid with silver frills at the shoulders. I also seemed like an animated doll with lips dappled in pink. He was constantly checking me while I was getting ready in the dressing room. I asked him with naughty expression, 'Are you looking for someone?' His fingers played with my wavy shinning curly hair.

'Baby, do you love me?'

I was smiling. He asked again, 'Do you love me?' I replied, 'Yes.'

He smiled and said, 'I know you love me. But did you love someone else?'

There was silence. A pin-drop silence. His expression left only silence. He had put a paper in my hand, 'I found in your bag. You should be knowing this already.' And went onto the stage.

"As your dad said that I may not worth to afford you but you truly worth of this one. You have heard what your dad said and never understood my side. You have been raised by him so my praise for you didn't bother much. You made my life change as I have nothing to do by being self. You never know how much you mean to me because you never allowed me to express my feelings.

You showered hatred that even turned to more love towards you. You are the biggest surprise of my life. You are my sweetest girl. I have fallen in love with you for what you are. Just the way you are. You and I make sense is just a dream. I will alone cherish forever. You are my love. Just can't imagine you, being paired with someone. I envy Sam to have you in his life. This comes with pain to wish, 'Happy togetherness for you both."

I stood amid like a dead soul. The thumping clap noise was going on during the performance. The boys were extraordinary. Their vocals and instrumental music were making the audience cheer for them. There was scrap in my singing. I was undergoing an emotion that I never felt. I don't belong here. And even don't belong to him.

I stepped back to off stage. I cried hard. Every drop had unspoken pain. I hated being troubled by unfortunate love over the genuine soul.

I was shouldered by gentle hands. His touch was as kind as my love. Tears flowed like a storm. He looked into my eyes.

I replied, 'Please continue with the show.'

He said wiping my tears, 'I am here for you. Your Raj is there with you.' I was speechless. He told, 'Your king of music is always there for you.'

I said, 'You are Sam, not Raj. And please don't be him. And I am sorry for not talking about him.'

He replied, 'Oh that's his identity. Does his remembrance bother you? And do you let him go?'

'I had no idea what love is until I met him. At our first occurrence, I didn't know anything about him. I was a happy girl when he was around. He has feelings for me. He has feelings for his girl Cera too. So he doesn't want to take our relationship to marriage.'

Sam gave close expression, 'Do you think marriage is must when you are in a relationship with the one who loves you beyond that commitment.'

I replied, 'If there is something more to love is nothing but marriage.'

He paused and said, 'I believe in love but I don't believe in marriage. I feel it breaks the bonding of love.'

I was shocked to hear from him. He continued, 'When dad told that you should get married, I was annoyed as he knows I am a person who hates to get into the institution of marriage. I don't like to be married. Somehow he always wanted me to lock here by putting responsibilities. So I replied upfront, "No dad." After repeating this exercise several times one day he spoke, "Are you fine to get married to Sonu?" He asked with smiles. I didn't take time to say, "Yes" because I am in love with you & the way you are. Since childhood, I know you as a person. So I don't want to lose you in my life. I don't have guts to say to your dad nor mine that I will be living with Sonu without being married. He showed loving gesture, 'Now, I am confessing than my beliefs, you are very important. I can't let you go from my life. And here is the commitment to marry you.' And held my hands, 'You mean a lot babe. If I am not feeling my mom's absence that is because of you.'

I said, 'I am with you, Sam. I am there for you.'

'Dude why did you disappear. Hey, you also. What happened to you

guys. Listen we got $ 5000 extra earnings.' Sam said, 'Should celebrate this dude.'

Jose smiled. They went onto the dais to receive the cheque. I was so happy to see Sam. His eyes were sparkling with the lights. I was called. I also held it. We then took a group photo, I being in the middle. This time Sam was next to me holding my hand.

******

In the Mumbai airport, at the conveyor belt, he said that woman is constantly looking at you. Damn even I don't look at you like that. I took a turn to see her.

'I am glad that I'm able to meet you again.' She said with a hearty smile and introduced her son.' And she looked at Sam.

I told, 'He is my fiancée.'

She said, 'She is the sweetest girl I have met.' And took my contact and

gave her address details to visit her home.

Sam asked, 'Who is she?'

I said we met in travel and had to fight to make management agree for her stuff which she carried in her handbag.

He said, 'Miss India, you fought with air India for her. What made you stand on her side?'

'Just my instincts.'

He replied, 'You are a strong protagonist.'

'I'm not this person. With the incidents happening in my life, I have become one.' And said, 'Raj is one of the reasons.'

'You are making me remember something. When dad asked, what made you quit Stanford. Do you think that your music is supreme than your education?'

I replied, 'My instincts said you will be a better person one day.'

'If I would have not quit I could be a different person but not the desired person of me.'

I smiled and said, 'Sometimes, it's good to follow your heart and do what it says.'

'You are here uncle.'

'Yes, beta from a long time.' And he looked at Sam.

'Because of him, it is usually waiting at the Airport. You are to make him responsible.'

'Dad, what did you say?'

They argued till we reached my compound.

Uncle said, 'Come home beta. Sam will cook for us.'

I smiled. He said, 'Shaadi ke dates baki hain. hum sochenge.' I told, 'Uncle lets discuss that in dad and mom's presence.'

At home, bro was there preparing for his mains. He spoke with hatred, 'You are engaged without my presence. I hate you.' I asked, 'You didn't wish me on my birthday.'

He replied with attitude, 'This is called nullification.'

'Acha! Do well in your exams. You should keep our family's pride.' He said, 'I am not Sam.'

I gave a strange look. He reacted, 'I heard this from Mom. She spoke a

hundred times about her son-in-law that he is our family's pride.' I asked, 'How about dad?'

'He is casual but whenever mom speaks he also adds his. I am fed up

with their praises. You know they have become mad about Sam.'

'Oh!' I said and entered my room. I set the bed cover. It showed glimpses of my emotions. It had equally toiled like me. It said last time when you wept, I absorbed your pain. I was wet but didn't complain at you.

'My dear sis, he yelled your phone is making sound.'

I said, 'Bring it to me.'

He replied, 'I can't. My focus will go.' I said, 'At least check, who's that?' He replied, 'Isha'.

I went with a rush.

He told, 'Call is cut. Does she knows, you are engaged?.' I said, 'No' and dialled her immediately.

She was screaming without any break. I couldn't understand, what she was saying. There was a change of voice, 'Hello girl?'

'Hey, model. How are you?'

'I am freaking awesome. I and Ankur are getting married. I am happy to call you for my wedding. I expect your presence.'

I replied, 'Buddy Congratulations! Thanks for the invite.'

'Awe! You and Isha are my dear ones. How can I miss you guys?'

I added, 'Convey my regards to Ankur.'

She said, 'Yeah. You know he has broken his leg. He should be recovering by then.'

I said, 'Oh so sad.'

She reacted, 'Hilarious. Every time he tried impressing me has affected his calf bone. I don't pity his situation rather enjoy it, unlike any other girlfriend.'

I laughed at her. 'Bro was irritated, 'What's going on there. Could you please control yourself.'

I asked her, 'So how did you fall in love?'

She was excited to talk about it, 'This guy regularly visits my bar. I used to attend him as a dear client. One fortunate night, I was planning to close the restaurant. He was there for late hours. I never ask my customers to leave. That day I did because I had a modelling assignment. The next day, early morning shoot. I see him almost everyday. So, mentioned politely, 'This is the closing time.' I gently showed

gesture to move.

He left with smiles on his face. After winding up the things, I came out.

He was struggling with his leg.'

I asked him, 'Do you need my assistance?'

He nodded his head. I saw him. He was staring at my eyes. I asked,

'What happened?'

He said, 'I follow your shows.'

I replied helping him to walk, 'Ooh!' And said, 'Something fell from your jacket.'

He then checked his pockets and mentioned, 'These are your sizzling captures.'

I was stunned.

'So were you waiting to hand over?' He smiled. And then later we were meeting often at my restaurant. One fine day we have decided to get married.

I then said to Isha, 'I am engaged to Sam. Both our families are very happy with this.'

She reacted, 'Sweetheart, it's your life to decide whom to couple. My opinion for Raj will never change. He is a loving partner.' And she closed the call.

Subhodhayam! Subhodhayam! Bro said they returned from their visit. I was in a low mood with little open eyes I said I know can hear mom's voice. Then she came, 'Get up fast Sam is here.'

I did fresh up to meet him. He was in tuff rugged pants. He rolled his eyes onto my mobile through my eye contact. There was a text dropped from him let's go out I need to talk to you.We moved out walking on the wet grass he mentioned, 'New York is calling me.'

I was shocked and uttered, 'What?' He replied, 'Maybe for a few days.'

I said, 'Anything in specific?'

He added, 'I want to visit for the last time. If dad knows this, he may feel I am staying back. You should manage that I am with you in your city.'

But I would be here in Mumbai.

He asked, 'Why? How about your work?'

I said, 'It's all because of the past. Don't want those redos.'

'Babes you should be rejoicing. I will make you forget the pain shadowing you.'

He was coming close. Then I looked into his eyes. He was blushing. I loved it.

'So you have asked me to come out to tell this. Only this.' He was blushing more.

I said, 'Just want to know.'

He replied, 'What do you mean babes?' I told, 'You know what I meant.'

He replied, 'We will go now dad would have come by now.'

We both were on leather couch while Raman uncle spoke, 'Pandith Ji said coming 16th Sep is an auspicious day.'

Sam replied, 'Dad why so quick.'

Even Sania's wedding falls on the same week I said to Sam. He whispered, 'Cool baby this date I will not be in India.'

I winked with a silent smile, 'I can marry another on the same date.'

His face has become pink like a puppy. He said, 'I am skipping my visit.'

I smiled more. Dad asked, 'Are you done with the whispers? Just tell us can we go ahead with this date.'

Sam replied holding my hand, 'Yes uncle' and said looking at me I will not take a risk. And then he spoke to Dad about my back to work. His words did magic. He is like a premium brand to them. They feel having him is a pride to the family.

I went to the office directly after my morning flight. I urged to unlock my computer. I composed an email stating went on an emergency vacation. I relieved once I clicked on the send button. Megha was there in the pantry stirring green tea bag in hot water. She looked at me twice with a surprise.

Hey you? What no notice? I heard you are engaged officially.

I asked, 'Did Ikya say you this?'

Yeah, she said. And you know my dear partner quit our company for an abroad opportunity.

I asked, 'In a short time this did happen.'

Yup, we were missing you on her last day. She was emotional to move out.

I replied, 'Miss her too. And said I will occupy her place.' She smiled, 'You can and I will have some company beside.'

I shifted my stuff to Vaidhya's place. I didn't find Ikya after passing time for hours. So checked where is she?

Megha replied, 'You didn't notice. Sometime back she went to Raj's room.'

'What?' whose?' I reacted like a thunder.

You should be remembering the pranks we did to our phone friend. That macho voice is in office. A week ago a lady visited. Her height equalled him. A girl as tall as a towering guy is rare. Her English speech did spell more like Spanish.

'He is here. Let me Leave' I uttered and stood up.

She said, 'Yeah let's go. I will introduce you as I get a chance to see him.'

She then pulled me down and said, 'Look they are coming out.' Raj noticed and stopped at our bay. Megha was excited for no reason. She did a big struggle stammering my name.

He helped her saying, 'Sonu' and said, 'Have seen the mail you dropped in the morning. You are very much welcome anytime.' I didn't reply.

He said, 'You always have that privilege.'

Megha continued to show excitement. He backed with a smile asked,

'Time for coffee?'

She acknowledged and stood close to him. He moved an inch from her and didn't stop staring at me.

She interrupted him saying, 'Shall we go. Sonu doesn't drink.' That left disappointment on his face.

Ikya greeted with a smile and asked, 'Are you happy with your life' I replied with confidence, 'Yeah.'

'But he is not. His love is unconditional. You will be losing such a lovable man.'

I questioned her directly, 'Would you be fine if your guy is having a relationship with some other girl.'

Her reply was, 'I don't hold his freedom.'

'Ikya, I know why you said this. And to this reason, you didn't speak about him to me.'

******

Sep 10^(th)

A sudden phone call has changed my life. I had to leave my marriage shopping cart in the middle. I rushed home.

I reacted to dad, 'What's wrong?'

From his static posture, Dad responded, 'Everything Sam did is intentional.'

Raman uncle was off. His first sentence to me, 'Sorry beta. I know about my son. But never thought that he would do this in the last moment. I will never forgive him and don't ever trust him. I felt your bonding will change him. But he is the same.'

I was holding my breath, controlling my feelings. I asked dad, 'I want to talk to Sam.' He showed silent gesture and immediately took me out.

I looked at him and asked, 'Please tell me what happened?'

He then spoke, 'Sonu.' With a gentle tone he said again, 'Sonu beta, life goes eventually not accordingly. Last night, I received a call from City hotel. His voice was broken. Completely shattered. I wanted to shut the line. He said, "Please listen to me, uncle. All that you are expecting from me is to marry Sonu. I am ready to give that commitment."

'Dad, suddenly how did I become his priority?'

'Beta, 'Cera is in Raj's life but she is not his love. And I could sense that his life is broken without you.'

'Dad, I don't want to be wrong twice. I thought Sam is the right one but don't tell me that it is again a mistake. Now it's all about my decision. And you get me married to Sam.'

'Beta, Sam broke the marriage.'

'What are you saying, Dad? He will never do that. He knows, I love

him. He gave his commitment.'

'I am sorry beta. He did it for your love.'

'Dad, are you listening. Sam is my love. Let me talk to him.' And I picked my mobile. He didn't attend my calls.

I texted, 'Pick up the damn phone.' He said, 'Hello.'

I asked, 'Why did you fail your promise?'

His voice spoke, 'Sonu your love will be back to you.' And there was silence.

I grieved, 'You don't care my feelings. I am in love with you.' Silence

maintained.

'Why Sam? Why are you so silent?.' He then disconnected the call.

Dad patted my back, 'I always want you to be happy. So I wish you to be with Raj.'

It was too painful. How can dad be so selfish playing with my emotions?

I didn't care anything, travelled to Delhi. I will not lose Sam for any. A big shock. he wasn't there at the musical performance. And suddenly on my right, a person moved too close to me. It's a familiar touch. I turned saw a pale face.

'Why are you here?'

He replied, 'I know you will come.'

'But I don't want to see you. I am here for my Sam.'
'He is not there. He doesn't want you anymore.'

'Don't dare to lie, how did you know?' 'He told me.'

'Why the hell, he will tell you?'

'Sweetheart, you are his best buddy, not his love.'

'Raj, just because you wanted me in your life don't speak rubbish.'

'Listen, after Sam had come from South Africa he met me. During the concert, he realized you have feelings for me. He confessed his love is out of need, fearing that he would lose you. True love is something that happens with no selfish reasons. Knowing my love for you, he wanted to convince your family, dropping the marriage. He also understood your dad mistook Cera's relationship. She was in psychological trauma, went into severe depression after her parents committed suicide. I had to be with her to make her come out of depression. She badly needed my presence. So I was living with her. She is as important as you but as a good friend. She is my true companion. So never left her in pain.' 'You guys don't mind my opinion? Don't you think I do have feelings?'

******

Sept, 16-Present day.

After Isha's phone, I heard a double knock with a solitude tone, 'Baby.'

I was yet to dress up in my bridal wear. I opened the door. I saw him

in Indian Dhoti. His reaction, 'Just can't believe this is happening.' I said, 'I always dreamt of this day as a child.'

He then gave a tight hug and told, 'You are the best thing of my life.' I told, 'You are my love.'

His eyes were wet that brought tears in my eyes.

Isha's voice was heard at the door, 'Buddy still struggling with the attire?'

He said, 'Nah Nah, I never tried this dhoti but I am absolutely fine to carry it.'

'Sam If I am not wrong, you and Raj have the same bracelet which is considered as an ancestor's blessings for Sonu's groom.'

'Isha, bracelets might be the same but the wrist she chose to walk along is only one.'

The macho voice said, 'Having the same will not make me Sonu's groom, loving her makes me the one.' And he expressed holding my hand.

Love is when you can't express your feelings while your partner understands it.

Love is when you are at discomfort your partner makes it ease.

Love is when you are at silence, your partner gently wakens your conscience to make you move.

Love is not just about missing your partner. It is also the feeling of their absence while they are far. I could feel his love. I looked into his eyes.

He said, 'Your mom has put it on my wrist.' I smiled, 'This is our family's pride.'

Isha expressed to him, 'You are the pride and to your love, Sonu is the perfect bride.'

Milton Keynes UK
Ingram Content Group UK Ltd.
UKHW031124261124
451618UK00005B/25